Ellen Olney Kirk

A Revolutionary Love-Story and the High Steeple of St.

Chrysostom's

Ellen Olney Kirk

A Revolutionary Love-Story and the High Steeple of St. Chrysostom's

ISBN/EAN: 9783744708098

Printed in Europe, USA, Canada, Australia, Japan

Cover: Foto ©Andreas Hilbeck / pixelio.de

More available books at **www.hansebooks.com**

A Revolutionary Love Story
and The High Steeple of
St. Chrysostom's

A Revolutionary Love-Story

and

The High Steeple of

St. Chrysostom's

BY

Ellen Olney Kirk

HERBERT S. STONE & COMPANY
CHICAGO & NEW YORK
MDCCCXCVIII

A Revolutionary Love-Story

" The course of true love never did run smooth."

ONE Sunday morning in July, 1776, Cicely, only daughter of John James Farrington, Esq., of Saintford-on-the-Sound, was standing before the oval mirror of her dressing-table, tying on her bonnet to go to church. She wore a gown of white paduasoy, embroidered with rose buds, over a bodice of sprigged muslin. Her large flaring bonnet of fine Leghorn straw was trimmed with a scarf of the silk, while inside the brim a cap of shirred

I

net framed the delicately featured
face. If Cicely Farrington was not
perfectly beautiful, she still possessed
many distinct traits of beauty. Her
eyebrows, her eyelids, the way the
dark hair grew away from her forehead
and temples; the modeling of her lips,
her hands, her feet: her slim shape and
nymph-like carriage — each of these
different points was in its way almost
perfect. At this moment, nevertheless, she surveyed her own charming
image without any satisfaction in herself or in her toilet. For in these
"times which tried men's souls"—

"To be drest
As you were going to a feast"

showed a dangerous leaning. Still, it
may be that Cicely cared less for public
than for private censors, or that what

she dreaded was lest a certain pair of eyes might be better pleased with Ruth Gentry in patriotic homespun than with Cicely Farrington in imported silk.

A knock at the door roused her from her reverie.

"Mars' Farrington says he's ready to 'tend Missus Cicely to church," called one of the black boys, indifferently trained to take the place of footman in the colonial establishment. And Cicely, with a glance back over her shoulder, hurried from her room and down the stairway.

Four men, hat in hand, stood ready to receive her.

"There is no haste, my daughter," said the squire, as John James Farrington was generally called. He was a man of sixty-four, tall and broad, and,

3

with his own gray hair tied in a queue, showed an old-world air of stateliness, further set off by his Georgian frock-coat, ruffled shirt and kneebreeches. His two sons, James and Bicknell, resembled him, and wore their nankeens and carried their three-cornered hats with rather a foppish air. The fourth of the group, a kinsman of Cicely's mother (now some ten years deceased), Morris Marshall by name, was dressed in a suit of rough gray homespun.

Marshall, in spite of a slight deformity which made him walk with a limp, was a powerful-looking man, with a cool, determined face, a subtle blue eye, an aquiline nose, a well-cut mouth and heavy jaw, all aided by a manner which gave his least word and act impressiveness. As the girl reached the lowest stair, he took a step forward and made a low salutation.

"You look like a bride, fair Cicely," he said, with an emphasis which seemed almost irony. "Will you go to church with me?"

"With my father, if it pleases you, Cousin Marshall," Cicely replied, with a slight rise of color in her cheeks.

"You do not like my homespun?"

"My Cousin Marshall is best judge whether he should wear homespun or broadcloth," Cicely said again, with a slight touch of disdain.

"Lay my fault to the emptiness of my pockets and the necessities of the times, Cousin Cicely," Marshall replied, with his easy air of dominating the situation. "I am glad, however, to keep a friend at court, while it may be well if the Farringtons have an humble kinsman and servant in homespun among the Sons of Liberty."

Cicely glanced at her father with some alarm at these political allusions, but Mr. Farrington only pursed his lips as he offered his arm to his daughter, and led the way through the great door, held wide open by two black servants, one on each hand, bowing obsequiously. Although the Farringtons had lived for more than a century in the Connecticut colony, the family had retained not only the traditions of high life in England, but in some reduced, scanty sort, many of its forms. John James Farrington himself, although born in Saintford of a father also born in Saintford, took a tone, and, it might also be said, wore an air of exile.

At this moment, as the knot of loungers gathered in front of the church caught sight of the advancing group of Farringtons, followed by their dog Ponto, Uriel Coxe, the wag of the village, exclaimed just above his breath:

"Here comes my Lord Farrington, born three thousand miles from his native land."

An unusual number of loungers had gathered in the wide, grassy street, a convenient place of reconnoissance for both houses of worship, one standing at the foot and the other on top of the slight eminence called "Meeting-house Hill." A feeling that something was about to happen was in the air. The crisis had been slow in reaching Saint-

7

ford, but it had come at last. While Massachusetts had been for years in rebellion against tyrannical governors and their edicts, active oppressions had so far galled and fretted the people of Connecticut very little. The old charter of 1662, the freest ever granted by royal favor, had enabled the colonists to go on electing their own governors and making their own laws, and in spite of their sympathy toward their sister colonies in revolt, the old feeling toward the mother country had long retained its efficacy. Saintford, for example, was a settlement of pure-blooded Englishmen, many of them of good position and substantial means, likely to think twice before flinging to the winds all that they had reverenced and clung to all their lives. The battle of Lexington had nevertheless been an imperious call summoning Major Marrable, his son Sidney and two or three others to action, and their example had gradually influenced public opinion and brought it up to the hostile point. By this time even those who most loved ease and a safe place at the fireside had become energetic opponents of the king's policy. Some three weeks before, the Connecticut legislature had ordered the king's name struck off legal and commercial paper; ten days later the congressional delegates had been instructed to support a declaration of the independence of the colonies, and on July fourth this had been signed in behalf of the state by Roger Sherman, Samuel Huntington, William Williams and Oliver Wolcott.

The gun of rebellion had been fired, yet on this pleasant Sunday morning the good Episcopalians of Saintford were wending their way to church to pray, as they had prayed all their lives, for the welfare of the royal family. Parson Kneeland had so far answered all expostulations in the matter by saying that he could not depart from rubric and ritual without orders from his bishop.

It was a beautiful day, and Saintford was a pretty village, with streets sixteen rods wide, set off by groups of trees of various foliage belonging to the original forests, not yet displaced by the regular rows of elms to be planted a little later and to become the crowning glory of the place. The church, dating back to 1743, was of imposing dimensions, with ample windows, comfortable pews, and a gallery with an organ; its tall steeple was surmounted by a richly gilded St. Peter's cock, veering to every breath of wind. The belfry contained a bell of unusual size and excellence of tone.

The plain, square Puritan house of worship stood, as has been said, not far away, and when the two bells, alternately pealing, answered each other, it was a saying of Uriel Coxe's that the meeting-house bell, small, ill-cast, ear-piercing, called out

O-rig-i-nal Sin! O-rig-i-nal Sin! O-rig-i-nal Sin!

while the church bell, deep, sustained, sonorous, made response—

Good old English roast beef! Good old English roast beef!

Mr. Farrington, his daughter and sons took all eyes as they passed on to the large square pew at the right of the chancel, and more than one prim glance grew more prim at sight of Mistress Cicely's brave apparel. The Continental Congress had urged frugality of dress upon all patriots, and the Sons and Daughters of Liberty had made a league to wear only homespun stuffs. Still, it had to be confessed that there was more ostentation in the way little Ruth Gentry presently followed Cicely up the aisle in a gown of linen, bleached whiter than snow, with a stiffened hat of the same material, wound round with a scarf of the finest, sheer-

12

est lawn, than in all Cicely's rich attire. Ruth, with coquettish challenge, seemed to say: "I spun and wove all that I have on from head to foot. Look at me, and see if I am not as fine a lady, besides being a prettier girl than Cicely Farrington."

Cicely yielded the palm of beauty on the spot. She blushed in shame at her own finery as she saw Ruth, shining like a gem out of her plain setting, pass to the end of the Marrables' pew. She hardly dared look to see who followed, but it was Madam Moulthrop, in her stiff-hooped brocade, with a black footman carrying her prayerbook, who rustled up the aisle after Ruth. Next came Major Marrable, lately returned from the expedition to Canada. He wore a sword, and when the haughty Tory dame, hearing it clank, turned sharply round to discover what the sound was, the scabbard caught in the lace that trimmed her petticoat. At thus encountering the most pronounced of all Saintford's rebels, Madam Moulthrop grew as red and fierce as a turkey cock, angrily caught her raiment away from the contamination of a rebel sword, and huddled into her pew, clanging the door as if barricading herself against an enemy.

Major Marrable stood aside, bowing with a deprecating air of concern for Madam Moulthrop's discomfiture, but he smiled nevertheless, and there was a look of amusement on many faces in the congregation. He waited for his son Sidney, a handsome young fellow in regimentals, to pass him, then both

sat down in the front pew with Ruth
Gentry (a cousin of Mrs. Marrable's,
brought up like a daughter in the
house) facing the Farringtons. Just
at that moment Morris Marshall happened to be looking at Cicely. Seeing
her grow suddenly rosy red, he turned
and caught the eager, devouring glance
Sidney Marrable had bent upon her.
Marshall's brow grew black. He all
at once understood why his own suit
to Cicely was rejected and disdained.
The sudden suspicion that Cicely cared
for her childish playmate struck like a
lash across the man's tenderest feelings.

Sidney Marrable was like Cicely, just
one and twenty. He had been a student at Yale College, when, after the
battle of Lexington, Benedict Arnold
mustered a company on the New Haven

green to march to Boston and join the patriots. Sidney had been in service of one sort or another ever since. He had fought under Ethan Allen at Ticonderoga, had followed Benedict Arnold into the wilderness and through the fruitless siege of Quebec. He had now, for some months, been at General Washington's own orders, for the commander-in-chief had at once recognized under the young fellow's light-hearted audacity, substantial qualities which justified the confidence reposed in him by each officer he had so far served. Sidney was hardly old enough for any considerable promotion, but he had held more than one detached command, where he had been conspicuous for enterprise and success. He had also shown capacity in certain separate and responsible services, when he had to see, hear, judge and act for his superiors. At this very time he was taking Saintford on his way back to headquarters, after a conference with General Wooster, stationed at Danbury, respecting certain reinforcements for the commander-in-chief, although the ostensible reason for his coming home was to meet Major Marrable, who was spending a brief furlough with his wife before rejoining General Gates.

The elder Marrable and Mr. Farrington had not been friends since the first mutterings of trouble began in the colonies. Major Marrable had attempted to instruct, not to say dictate to, the squire, as to the direction in which his duty lay. At this moment

17

2

each of the two men betrayed his consciousness of the other's proximity by a certain stiffening of mien.

The bell stopped tolling almost as soon as the Marrables had taken their seats. At the first note of the organ, the door of the vestry-room, which was situated at the entrance to the church, opened, and the Reverend Ebenezer Kneeland, with his lawn surplice flying out a yard behind him, came swinging up the long, broad aisle to the reading-desk. His face was pale and showed a compressed lip and twitching nostril. As he rose from his knees, after a moment's silent prayer, his eyes traveled boldly round the church; then opening the great folio prayer-book, he read the opening sentence:

"When the wicked man turneth away

from his wickedness, that he hath committed, and doeth that which is lawful and right, he shall save his soul alive."

His glance encountered the straight, commanding gaze of Major Marrable, who looked not only alert, but primed for action. The clergyman waited a moment, then gathering himself together afresh set forward to read the invocations and prayers with a mighty ardor. The responses were as fervent. It was as if the spirit had descended not only upon the pastor, but upon his people. The Venite and Benedictus, sung by all who chose to join, gained extraordinary volume. The Te Deum was uplifting in its majestic flow; the creed, as it rang forth, suggested the crossing of drawn swords. Then began the litany, and into every peti-

tion was poured an eloquence of suppli-
cation which left few eyes dry.   A
subtle, indescribable sense of the significance of passing events had its
clutch upon each individual consciousness.

"Remember not, Lord, our offenses,
nor the offenses of our forefathers,
neither take thou vengeance of our
sins; spare us, good Lord, spare thy
people, whom thou hast redeemed with
thy most precious blood, and be not
angry with us forever."

Then the response, "Spare us, good
Lord," came with sobs.

It was as if into the hearts of all was
poured a sudden illumination of what
this prayer might come to mean.   Parson Kneeland was never again to kneel
in that familiar place.   Not until after

the close of the war were prayer and praise again to go up in this Saintford church. And as if each thought had its imagination in the future, the suspense, the dread, the suffering human need of help not from flesh and blood; the agony of partings, the pang unassuaged and unassuageable for cruel loss which was to come, took voice and was poured out with irrepressible force of meaning.

"From battle and murder and from sudden death"—

"Good Lord, deliver us."

"From all sedition, privy conspiracy and rebellion"—

said Parson Kneeland, with peculiar emphasis, and the senior warden's voice answered sonorously,

"Good Lord, deliver us."

"In all time of our tribulation, in all time of our wealth, in the hour of death and in the day of judgment"—

"Good Lord, deliver us."

"We sinners do beseech thee to hear us, O Lord God, and that it may please thee to rule and govern thy holy church universal in the right way."

"We beseech thee to hear us, good Lord."

The Reverend Mr. Kneeland had grown very pale. He opened his lips once in vain, then struggling to command his voice and fluttering heart-beats, he broke forth:

"That it may please thee to keep and strengthen in the true worshiping of thee, in righteousness and holiness of life, thy servant GEORGE, our most gracious King and Governor——"

22

There was a rustle and stir. Some of the men in the congregation were rising from their knees. One man was on his feet. His voice rang out like a shot:

. "I protest," said Major Marrable.

White faces looked up. Mr. Farrington was struggling to rise, but his sons held him down in his seat, and Cicely clung to him, hiding her face.

Parson Kneeland, as if he would not let himself hear, but must press on, began—

"That it may please thee——"

"Stop!" thundered Major Marrable, with a face hardening to flint. The clergyman, slowly and shakily, as if benumbed, rose from his knees and stood staring.

"In the name of our liberties, for which we have to struggle," said Major

Marrable, "in the name of the homes we have to protect, in the name of the Commonwealth of Connecticut and of the Continental Congress, which has declared our independence of Great Britain, I *protest*, as senior warden of this church, against prayers being offered at this altar for George the Third, who is not our friend, who has proved himself our bitter enemy."

Parson Kneeland was a tall man. At this moment he towered up above the congregation like an awful accusing angel, a frown gathering on his brow, his eyes flashing lightnings of wrath.

His right hand, until now resting under the heavy cover of the great folio prayer-book, lifted it and brought it down with a crash, closing that page forevermore.

Then he flung up both hands, and held them hovering tremulously over his people, while, bending forward, he gave the benediction.

"The grace of our Lord Jesus Christ and the love of God and the fellowship of the Holy Ghost be with us all evermore.   Amen."

II

THE parson knelt one instant, then sprang up, and with great strides took his way down the aisle, his surplice floating far behind him, and, not even stopping to enter the vestry, walked straight out of the church and home to the parsonage.

His congregation watched him depart with trouble and confusion. Madam Moulthrop, who had burst into cries and sobs, was led to her coach by James Farrington. The squire, maintaining a lofty demeanor, offered one arm to his daughter, but on the other side he was glad to accept the support of his son

Bicknell. Morris Marshall, whose face had worn a look of half-malign enjoyment of the scene, stayed behind to put a few questions to Major Marrable and to exchange greetings with Ruth Gentry.

Sidney Marrable had followed just behind Cicely Farrington, as she went down the aisle clinging to her father, but he had not ventured to address her. She was strangely shaken and at the mercy of conflicting ideas, but he had one glance from her full of touching reproach.

"They have robbed me of my country, they have robbed me of my king, and now they have robbed me of my church," said the old man, as he sat down in his own seat at home in an attitude of profound dejection.

"But not of our God," said Cicely.

"He is with us. He sees. He knows.
He has patience. Let my dearest father
try to wait and look beyond these hap-
penings."

Mr. Farrington shook his head, and
remained unconsoled by his daughter's
words. Morris Marshall, entering presently, tried his best to make clear to the
squire the far-reaching significance of
the political situation. Marshall, who
had large estates near White Plains,
after halting and debating for some
months, had of late espoused the cause
of the patriots. He was a man apt to
study his own profit, and had not cut
himself off from the older cause out of
any mere glow of enthusiasm for the
new. Indeed, the immediate future of
the patriots looked to him very dark,
but he knew that the emphatic revolt

of the colonists was the manifestation
of something in these men that the
mother-country ignored and outraged.
Why had men emigrated and settled
America except that they were conscious of a new fiber in their moral
being which made them eager for free-
dom, for room to expand each at his
own need and in his own way? That
leaven was still working, and must
work. It was indestructible.

To Mr. Farrington, however, the
lawless and riotous conduct of these
demagogues, as he called the men who
were trying to turn the world upside
down, was a matter of mortification,
grief and bewilderment. It seemed to
him the basest ingratitude for the
colonists, after accepting every sort of
benefit from the royal hand, sordidly to

refuse to pay just and equitable taxes. "Blind, blind, blind! they little know the fate that is before them," that was Mr. Farrington's refrain. They were sowing the wind, and presently would reap the whirlwind—black, bitter, final. Such a triumph as Major Marrable had just scored was to the squire the triumph of gross license over everything worthy and sacred.

Morris Marshall set himself the task of combating this state of mind. Major Marrable, on returning to Saintford, had been appealed to by different members of the vestry, and had told Parson Kneeland that the prayers for George the Third and the royal family must no longer be read, and Parson Kneeland had replied that it was for him to obey his bishop according to the

canons of the church, and that he could
not make over the prayer-book to suit
the heresies and assumptions of an
unscrupulous, desperate and mischiev-
ous faction.

"There are some men so blind,"
observed Morris Marshall, "they will
not see what is taking place before their
eyes. What would the parson think of a
seaman who, setting forth from port with
a fair wind, will not alter his course if
it changes, trim his sails and avoid
meeting the tempest in its teeth?"

Mr. Farrington and his eldest son
were, however, for sailing against the
wind. A man could not serve two
masters; acknowledge both a higher
and a lower law.

Marshall answered that it was useless
to maintain an arbitrary and despotic

tone about the colonists. It was as well to consider the stuff of which they were made. Happy, prosperous, contented men were not the class that had emigrated. The Old World had planted her dragon's teeth in these colonies. The men were born to love fighting; they were ready to fight anything, questions of free-will and predestination, the form of baptism, Indians, witches, stamp-acts, governors and their edicts —above all, the king's soldiers. Everything with these New Englanders was a matter of conscience, and in their own way and their own time they must work out their own salvation.

"Their own destruction and the destruction of all connected with them," the squire returned, with an air of washing his hands of their crimes.

While this talk went on, Cicely went and came, sometimes pausing to listen to her cousin Marshall. The first rush of indignation and alarm at the event which had disturbed the morning service had begun to give way to other feelings. When she heard Marshall say that instead of listening to the petitions of the colonists, instead of trying to understand their grievances, the British government answered them by still greater exactions, Cicely felt herself tingle with sudden patriotic fervor. She knew at the same moment that any withdrawal of her sympathy from his father's side would plant an arrow in his heart.

Torn this way and that, she went up to her own white dimity-hung room and fell on her knees by the bedside;

34

her hopes, fears, tremblings and long-
ings all merging into the prayer that
these troubles might pass—that all those
whom she loved might be safe and
happy again. While she still knelt
something near her seemed to move.
She looked up and lying close beside
her on the oaken floor was a three-
cornered billet sealed with scarlet
wax.

In all her life Cicely had known nothing clandestine, and at the sight of this
missive, which must have flown in at
the open window, she blushed like a
guilty thing. She looked round at the
closed door, started to her feet, stole to
the window, gave a frightened glance,
first at the grape trellis, then out into the
lawn and garden to see if anyone was
in sight. Nothing stirred in the Sunday

sunshine but the birds and the vagrant breeze wandering among the vines and flowers. Neither bird nor breeze could have brought the letter. Nevertheless Cicely was at no loss to know whence or how it had come. She opened it.

"I must have speech with Mistress Cicely. I came yesterday at sunset. I set out to-night, for I need to be at headquarters by noon to-morrow. After it grows dusk I shall be waiting under the willow trees. Will Mistress Cicely deign to meet her old friend in the old place? She knows that he who asks this favor asks it on his knees. She knows, too, that he would not ask it were he but free to knock at her father's door and have leave to enter."

Had anyone seen? Had anyone

36

heard? Cicely stole out and listened on the landing and heard one voice after the other of the four men rise from the discussion below in the hall. With a feeling of relief she now read the letter over again, seeming to hear Sidney's voice pleading, seeming to meet his smiling, tender, yet half-commanding look. Until to-day she had not even had a glimpse of him for more than a year. They had grown up together, played together, studied together. His own sense of possession in her was answered by every chord of feeling in her whole nature.

When presently she descended and took her place at the dinner-table Morris Marshall looked at her with a keen look of inquiry. He saw that something had happened within the last hour. She had been pale and drooping. Now she seemed to smile involuntarily, her eyes were wide open, their pupils dilated, and a soft pink flush suffused her cheeks. She had suddenly grown beautiful, but he knew by instinct that it was with a beauty not born for him. He grew silent and suspicious. He determined to watch her.

Matters of moment had been settled in the discussion before dinner. James, the eldest son, had come home from Oxford in June to see his father and to settle the question whether, in view of the approaching troubles, he might not better abide with his family. It was now decided that while there was yet time he should find an opportunity to return to England in one of the transports. Mr. Farrington offered the same

38

course to Bicknell, but the younger son was of a different mind.

Cicely looked from one to the other, mute. She was suddenly daunted by the practical difficulties which rose and confronted her. The contradiction between her childish romance and the trials and perplexities appointed to the woman suddenly showed a gap and chasm which made her tremble and shrink back.

Her silence passed unnoted, for it was her habit. When the cloth was drawn she left the four men over their port and madeira, from which, as the custom of the day was, they had not risen when at half-past six she brought them each a dish of tea, offering along with it bread and butter, dried cow's tongue and sweet biscuits. At half-

past seven came prayers for the house·
hold, always read in the evening by
Cicely herself. Her voice faltered a
little as she gave the petitions for the
royal family. Marshall, patriotic although he was, was also a man-of-the-
world, quarreled with no man's creed
in his own house, and accordingly gave
a sturdy "Amen."

Mr. Farrington sat nodding in his
chair after devotions were over. James
and Bicknell went out to tell Madame
Moulthrop the news and ask if she had
any commands for England. Marshall
had hoped that this distribution of the
family would give him a chance for a
quiet talk with Cicely, which was the
real object of his visit. What was his
chagrin, when long before half-past
eight o'clock, after giving him only a

distracted and divided attention, she rose, and pleading fatigue, asked her father's permission to retire to her room.

"I see no sleep in your eyes, fair Cicely," said Marshall, as he brought her candle, looking in her face with a smile of such ironic meaning that her glance fell beneath his. She blushed vividly. Her lips quivered. "It seems a pity to waste such bright looks on the darkness," he continued, his insatiable glance fastening on her lovely downcast face.

"I am very tired," she faltered. "I beg you will excuse me." She took the candle from him and went slowly up the stairs. Marshall's was a mind in which suspicion stirs vulpine insight. He stood for a moment watching the

girl until she vanished into the darkness, then making the remark to Mr.
Farrington that he would take a turn in
the garden, he left the house by the
back door of the hall which opened into
the court. The path from this led
toward the east. At the west end of the
large square colonial house was a long
low wing which contained the kitchen
and servants' quarters. Against this
wing rested the grape trellis, and in
the corner where wing and trellis joined
the main building was Cicely's room.
In this direction walked Marshall and
stood looking up. A light showed
through the white curtains which
swayed gently in the evening breeze.
As he still looked up a slight sound disturbed the stillness—not the chirp of an
insect or the note of a sleepy bird, but

the unmistakable click of a bolt shot in the little side door.

Marshall suffered as if he had been struck a blow. No one but Cicely could be leaving the house by that door, for it was always kept jealously locked and bolted, commanding, as it did, a private staircase. In another instant a tall, slim figure passed him like the wind. It was Cicely. She had thrown a dark cloak over her white gown, but still it was not wholly concealed. He could have put his hand on her as she flew along the grape walk.

He stood motionless, staring, thrilling as if under a supreme insult. He felt heartsick, cruelly humiliated. Then slowly his anger began to burn. He limped along the path the girl had so fleetly taken, saying within himself he

43

would follow her and put her to shame. He knew that it would count as a crime to all the Farringtons that Cicely should be stealing out like a kitchen-maid to meet any lover—but above all one of those seditious Marrables. For a moment Marshall knew but one feeling—that was a longing to reach the girl, strike her down, disgrace her.

Then his mood changed. He stopped short in his pursuit. With a shrug he recognized the folly of such violent emotions. Deciding to wait and watch the turn of events he returned to the house, entering by the secret door, and with a grim smile bolted it behind him. It was by this time nine o'clock. The young men had come in and were sitting with their father. In twenty min-

44

utes more the entire household save its youthful mistress was in bed.

Cicely, meanwhile, after flying down the trellis walk, had kept under the shadow of the garden wall until she reached an open space, across which she scudded, bending low until she reached the group of willow trees, which grew in a quiet corner of Mr. Farrington's home pasture, and also overhung the adjoining place, which belonged to Major Marrable. As she pushed aside the low hanging branches she paused and seemed afraid to advance. She was waited for. An arm was thrown round her; someone, bending over her, pressed a kiss on her forehead, then on her temples, at last on her lips.

She tried to escape, but that was nothing.

"Why, sweetest," he whispered, "it is I."

"Now, Sidney—"

"Now, Cicely—"

"But, Sidney—"

"But, Cicely! I am going to set out before midnight. I have not seen you for months and months. Heaven knows when I shall see you again."

"Oh, Sidney, my father is so angry with your father!"

"Your father is always angry with my father. It is for us to make up the love that is lost between them."

"It makes me feel the more how wrong, how wicked it was for me to come."

"It makes me feel the more your goodness in coming."

"I had no other way of answering your note."

"You did as you were bidden, sweet," he laughed. "You knew very well that either you had to come to me or I should have braved your father's wrath and gone to you."

In spite of the strength of the young fellow's impetuous clasp Cicely had by this time withdrawn from him. Her cloak fell to the ground and she stood before him touched by the low straight beams of the rising moon into luminous whiteness.

"Oh, you angel," he cried, ready to fall at her feet.

"How could your father break into the divine service?" Cicely now asked with passionate indignation. "Is nothing to be held sacred?"

"I told him to let the parson go on. George the Third needs the benefit of all the prayers we can offer for him, sinner that he is."

"Oh, Sidney!"

"It was the 'king and governor' that stuck in the throat. George the Third will never more be king or governor in this commonwealth."

"Oh, Sidney, you say such terrible things!"

"I mean to speak the truth, God help me."

"But I love England with all my heart."

"With *all* your heart, sweet?"

Cicely laughed slightly and leaned a little toward him as he clasped her hands.

"Ruth Gentry was telling me to-day that you cared only for England and that you would no doubt find a husband among the British officers who are coming over to coerce us."

"What did you tell her?"

"What did I tell Ruth? Do you suppose I could bring myself to say to her what I hardly dare say to myself in thought—that it is not a British officer you care for? Sometimes I pluck up a stout heart—I say to myself that by the time we have gained our liberties I hope to have something to offer you."

"Tell me what else Ruth Gentry said," murmured Cicely.

"It was an envious fling at your beauty so well set. She asked me if you ought to walk in silks and brocades as if you were going to court while good patriots are patiently pinching and saving for the cause."

"What answer did you make?"

49

4

"Cicely, I make no answer when Ruth and my mother find fault with you. They are jealous that when I come back I have hardly a word to utter, that good food might as well be thrown to the dogs as wasted on me;—that I lie tossing on my bed. To be within a few rods of you, yet not to be free to see you, to hear you, to touch even your hand, makes me ill company for those who like good meals and lively talk."

"But cousin Marshall was saying to-day that he saw signs of you and Ruth being lovers," faltered Cicely.

To find Cicely jealous gave Sidney the sweetest triumph of his life. It was the wish of his mother's heart that he should marry Ruth, who was a distant cousin and an adopted daughter, but he had always been in love with Cicely,

even while he knew that Mr. Farrington would consider it presumption that
the son of one of his plain neighbors
should raise his eyes to the only daughter
of his house. Now that the war had
come with its tangible rewards to strive
for, the young fellow's imagination
clapped its wings and soared.

"Ask your cousin Marshall what a
man is to do when a timid girl reaches
out her hand for protection," Sidney
now explained. "Ruth is my kinswoman, and I had not the wish nor the
will not to answer her appeal. She was
cruelly frightened when my father
spoke out. But Cicely—Cicely, surely
I do not need to tell you that she is only
my cousin, my adopted sister. Do I
need to swear on my knees that—"

"No, no, no," cried Cicely. "I am

not always as noble as I should be—and Ruth—Ruth is so pretty, so—''

"Do I wish to praise Ruth's beauty? Did I come here to talk about Ruth?''

"It is all my fault,'' murmured Cicely, stricken.

"Yes, it is all your fault that I care for no other girl under heaven save Cicely Farrington—that if I have a word of praise I think to myself, 'If Cicely could but hear this?' If my horse carries me well I say, 'I wish Cicely could see me.' When I seem to be in the way of advancement I dare think, 'It is all for Cicely.' Do you begin to know how I love you? Do you ever try to guess why I love you? It is partly because you just seem to belong to me, and partly too, because you are so fair, so divine, so grand a lady above them all. Cicely, oh, my beautiful Cicely, if I have something fully worth offering you, will you be my wife?"

Resisting ever so little his fervor she all the time withdrew from him. He could see her face, clear and pure in the white moonlight.

"I will be your wife," she said, with intense solemnity.

He fell on his knees before her. His tenderness overflowing.

"Oh, my wife, my wife, my wife," he murmured, lifting his hands in adoration. Her slim fingers fluttered into his. "Oh, I love your little hands— your little wrists. Oh, surely I worship you. Though I don't believe in kings, you are my princess, my queen! I grovel at your feet before you. I am kissing your buckles. Put your shoe on my neck. Let me feel myself your accepted vassal."

An irresistible little girlish laugh broke from Cicely. For one moment in her life, happy spontaneous girlish coquetry governed her mood. Romance, too, tinged her imagination. Light as thistledown her foot touched his neck.

"Rise, Sir Sidney Marrable," she said, gaily.

But her gaiety lasted only for an instant. The watchman's cry sounded from the street.

"Past ten o'clock. A fair, clear night, and all's well."

Cicely's heart began to beat with apprehension.

"I must go in," she said, with decision.

Yes, she must go in, but she was his

54

promised wife and parting was not too easy. What wonder if they still lingered under the grape trellis. He believed in the cause; he believed in its success; he believed in himself; he felt capable of carrying through whatever he undertook, yet perhaps within twenty-four hours he would be in battle.

"Good-by," she whispered, as they reached the little vine-covered doorway.

"I will wait until you wave to me from your window."

"Good-by," she said once more.

She drew the cloak closer about her. Her hand was on the latch of the door, which she had left ajar.

He could hear her pressing against the frame. Following her he tried his own strength.

"It is bolted," he said.

Something nameless and measureless seemed to draw near her and threaten. Who had bolted it? He was looking into her pallid face.

"The other doors are sure to be fastened?" he asked.

"Yes, and they are close under my father's and brothers' rooms."

She sank down on the step in agitation. The thought of her father, of her brothers, who had believed in her—who had looked up to her—showed her the fault she had committed.

For an instant Sidney's brain had whirled, then in a flash it cleared.

"Wait here one instant," he whispered. Even while he spoke he was pulling off his heavy riding-boots.

"What are you going to do?" she demanded, fearfully.

"Luckily, I knew the house. I have been up the trellis already once today."

The horror of those long minutes while she waited persisted like a physical chill for days afterward. She drew her breath in pain while Sydney, with the agile habit of the boy he really was, climbed up the trellis, the top of which was almost on a level with the window of Cicely's bedchamber. There was, however, a gap of some eight feet and this he had to leap. The lattice was, as usual, open to the summer air, and Sidney, raising his figure to its full height on the edge of the arbor, braced himself for the spring, then in another second was scrambling over the broad ledge.

Cicely was almost fainting when she heard the bolt pushed from inside.

The door opened. Sidney was bending over her.

"Sweetest, forgive me," he whispered, "but you will find a kiss from me on your pillow."

"Oh, Sidney, if you had met my father, my brothers!"

"I met nobody; and if I had, what matter? You are Cicely Farrington and I am Sidney Marrable."

He raised her hand to his lips, gently thrust her inside the door and closed it. He waited until he saw her figure at the window above, then drew on his boots, and prepared for his night ride back to General Washington's headquarters.

III

"PEACE hush this dismal din of
arms. January 4, 1778," Cicely
Farrington wrote with the diamond of
her mother's ring on one of the panes
of the window whose open casement
Sidney had entered that July night
long before.

The Revolutionary War has been matter of history for a century. Cicely's
vital frame was long since crumbled to
dust in the family vault at Saintford,
but still that passionate sigh of love and
longing and suspense makes its meaning clear as we trace those words on the

glass. We can fancy Cicely stealing up to the refuge of her room away from visitors who oppressed; from her father's querulous cravings and questionings, which she could not answer; from news which made her heart leap to her throat. There, she could always find a sustaining thought of Sidney Marrable. She had only to close her eyes to see the handsome young head, with its clustering curls, bending to kiss her pillow.

That incident had not been without its sequel.

When, on the Monday morning, she encountered Morris Marshall, she saw in his ironic smile, she heard in his mocking voice as he asked, "Did you sleep well, fair Cicely?" that he had her secret.

He had hardly reckoned on the girl's courage and spirit.

Her upper lip took an acute lift in its curve, the flash of her eyes went through him.

"It was my Cousin Marshall who bolted the little door last night," she said, with perfect steadiness. "God forgive him and give him a better heart." Their eyes met and she saw that the glance of the strong man faltered before hers. "You must have forgotten that I was the motherless girl of your dead cousin, that you are my father's guest—that I am your hostess."

For a moment Marshall, taken by surprise, was ready to be ashamed of the part he had played. Then the thought of the callow youngster preferred before him made him bitter.

"If I am your mother's cousin, your father's guest; if you are both my kinswoman and my hostess, I am the more jealous for your honor," he replied gravely. "Iachimo in my Imogen's bed-chamber—"

"My honor is not in the question," said Cicely. "I admit that I was foolish and imprudent to go out to see Sidney. Never before have I done such a thing, and this lesson has taught me never again to leave the safe shelter of my father's house. But these troubles have brought new times and new times have brought new manners."

"Say no more," cried Marshall, as if smitten with remorse. "Forgive the part I played—by chance. I give you my word, Cousin Cicely, that as I was returning from a stroll in the garden

I saw that the side door was open, and, supposing it had been left ajar for my convenience, I entered, fastening it behind me. I went to bed, but could not fall asleep. Then there came the sound of the latch being tried. I heard whispers outside. I rose, dressed, was about to descend, when I saw issuing from the door of your bedroom—"

"Sidney was my constant playmate," faltered Cicely. "As a boy he had climbed up that trellis again and again. He knows every inch of the house. He—"

"But if it had been your father, or one of your brothers, who saw him as I saw him—"

He looked at her blushing, troubled, tremulous face. He took her hand between his.

"We will think of it no more. I will

speak of it to no one," he said. Then as if to ratify his promise he bent his head and glued his lips to her hand.

She shrank from the caress, even while she gave him credit for magnanimity. She was grateful for his silence, for she realized almost painfully her own imprudence. She was at first inclined to be glad that Marshall at last knew that she had an accepted lover. She hoped that his long glances, his flatteries, his confidences would now cease. Cicely was to find out that she had given him certain intimate rights he had never ventured to claim before. Marshall was two-and-thirty years of age; so old, to Cicely's youthful imagination, that his wish to marry her seemed an unimportant factor in the situation. He had been in love with her ever since she was sixteen. He had an adroit way, when he passed the bounds of her concession, of suddenly effacing his passion, as it were, and becoming instead of a suppliant, with a soft pulse for charm and sweetness, an earnest man, bent upon important business, with little time or inclination for love-making. She realized very little of Marshall's pertinacity, and could still less have believed that his present patience was born of his hope that the chances of war would soon rid him of his rival.

The stream of events carried Marshall away from Saintford, and Bicknell Farrington with him. James had gone back to continue his terms in England. But the younger brother said to his father:

"I never was in England. So far as I know England never did anything for me. I was born here, and I expect to die here. You have always told me, sir, that a man ought always to be ready to fight for his country. I am going to fight for mine."

Marshall, although too severely crippled to be a soldier, had a brevet title, ranked as major, and had often served as a staff-officer. He had hoped and expected to find early promotion for Bicknell Farrington, but the poor boy was picked off by a shot from a picket while making a reconnoissance before the battle of White Plains. It· was Sidney Marrable who laid the dead boy across his own saddle and bore him back to camp. Sidney, broken-hearted at having done so little for Cicely's brother, for whom he had wished to do so much, flung himself on Morris Marshall's neck and cried like a child. He little guessed in what jealous wrath the emotion that convulsed the older man had its impulse. Marshall cried out against fate that the bullet had not found its billet in Sidney Marrable's breast instead of Bicknell Farrington's. Bicknell's life was desirable, while Marshall longed with an increasing passion of longing to see Sidney Marrable lie, stretched out white and rigid, staring up at the sky. It seemed impossible that any man who set so slight a value upon life as Sidney seemed to do should come out of the war in safety. He asked to be sent wherever there was to be fighting. General Washington had observed of the ambitious youngster that it was sometimes useful to have a man at one's elbow who did not know what "impossible" meant.

Bicknell had been deeply beloved and was deeply mourned at home. Saintford people might well grow more tender to the Farringtons now that they had given a son and brother to the cause of independence. Indeed, in their case, the hatred and suspicion often felt against tories had never defined itself into active hostility. It had even been considered charitable to wink at Parson Kneeland (he only survived the closing of his church two years) for reading prayers in Mr. Farrington's dining-room on Sunday mornings for the benefit of Madam Moulthrop and a few others. Most of the Saintford people attended the meeting-house nowadays. Cicely wrote to Sidney Marrable:

"Old Ponto is exercised in his mind because the church-bell is silent when the meeting-house bell rings. He walks forth on a Sunday, but when he beholds the people flocking up the hill, he sniffs with disdain and lies down on the mill-stone before the church door until he sees the neighbors go home again. He is neither Calvinist nor Puritan, not he. But oh, my friend, how long it seems since that Sunday morning."

"How long it seems since that Sunday evening, sweetheart," Sidney wrote back from the camp at Valley Forge. "But perhaps by the time we tell our children and our children's children what we have suffered, it will be clear to us that the sacrifice has not been in vain. The chaplain preached before his excellency last Sunday on the text, 'For I reckon that the sufferings of the present time are not worthy to be compared with the glory that shall be revealed to us.' Kiss the white spot on Ponto's head for me and tell him I love him for being faithful to church and king just as I love his mistress for being faithful to what she was brought up to reverence. Faith is not to be worn like the fashion of a hat that ever changeth with the next block, as we read in the play that day, sweet. Dost remember? Oh, to sit in a room warmed by a fire, to sleep in a bed beneath a roof, to eat food well cooked and well served. Seven of us lay on the ground last night with a little straw for softness and warmth under a tent six by seven—

stretched out like candles in a box, for we loved not our neighbors, and when one man got cramps the seven of us had to turn over, and as each man's cramps came at a different moment there were few intervals of peace and comfort. If one could always be going into battle with drums beating and flags flying it would be worth while being a soldier."

Cicely had not told Sidney that she had found it impossible since Bicknell was killed to say "Amen" when Parson Kneeland read the prayers for the royal family. The girl's tenderness and keen fellow-feeling for the absent might have drawn her toward Sidney's mother, but that good dame was no friend to Cicely. One day, however, when a neighbor had mentioned that if Sidney Marrable recovered from his wounds he

was likely to be promoted for his gallant conduct at the battle of Princeton,
Cicely was little more than a beating
heart and palpitating nerve until she
could set out to learn the truth. She
met Ruth Gentry issuing from Mrs.
Marrable's door.

"Miss Cicely Farrington coming to
visit plain patriots!" Ruth cried, raising her hands in mock surprise. She
stood on the stone steps dressed in
a heavy gray woolen homespun, with
a little close hood of the same edged
with squirrel's fur. Her bright rosy
cheeks, her laughing lips and eyes
made Cicely feel sad and old in com-
parison.

"Oh, Ruth," she faltered, reaching
out both hands, "I came to ask about
Sidney."

72

Ruth looked with surprise at Cicely's tearful, quivering face.

"What am I to tell you about Sidney?" she asked, with a little toss of the head.

"Is he wounded?"

"That was a month ago. I had a letter from him to-day."

"Oh, what did he say?"

Ruth bridled. "Do you suppose he would wish me to tell you?" she asked, with her coquettish air.

"Sidney and I are old friends," Cicely answered, recovering her self-command. "I only wish to be assured of his good health."

"He is well enough to be on the general's staff!" said Ruth, triumphantly —"his excellency the commander-in-chief's staff."

Snow covered the ground. The sky was gray, the horizon purple, more snow was to come and Cicely perhaps experienced its chill, for all the rest of that day and evening she felt benumbed and the sensation persisted of a cold clutch upon her heart. She was haunted by the recollection of Ruth's bright, piquant face. She would not permit herself to be jealous, but there was a passionate cry within her.

"He ought to have sent me word. If he could write to Ruth he could have written to me."

If she could have been permitted some intimate fellowship of feeling with Mrs. Marrable and Ruth! But they suspected her, disliked her, calumniated her.

It was well that Cicely had little time

for brooding over her separation from Sidney and her isolation among her neighbors. All her invention, skill, and resource were necessary to maintain the household on anything like its old basis of thrift, not to . say elegance. Money or bond brought in few and scant returns nowadays; rents were no longer paid, cargoes were lost or confiscated. The army commissariat, bare as it was, took up all available stores of medicine, food and forage. Instead of a houseful of black servants Cicely had but two inside and two outside, for two had gone with poor Bicknell and had stayed on; others had run away to follow the camps, where they found employment as cooks, body servants or orderlies. Mr. Farrington's energies were paralyzed by grief and bewilder-

ment. He seemed suddenly an old
man. Not only the supervision of the
house, but of the plowing, planting,
hoeing and harvesting came upon Cicely,
for never had the whole possible yield
of the farm and garden been needed as
now. It was Cicely who kept up the rear-
ing of beeves, pigs, fowls; who looked
to the killing and curing. The making
of maple sugar had become a matter of
importance; the preserving and drying
of fruit, in fact the converting of whatever product into what could serve as
food and drink was the foremost duty
of the moment. And in those early days
it might well be said that the fertile
earth had but to be scratched and seed
put in to laugh with teeming harvests.
The fruit trees, native and imported,
bent to the earth laden. The Farring-

ton storeroom and larder soon became the center of supplies for the village. Cicely had long since counted the dwindling bottles of port, madeira, sherry and cognac, and put them away. Who could tell what need might come for good wine? She brewed beer, made cider, cherry bounce, elder flower, blackberry and currant wine.

It was Mr. Farrington's one source of pride nowadays that Cicely kept up the traditions of the house, and flaunted, as it were, English thrift and plenty in the face of their neighbors, who lived from hand to mouth, yet foolishly went on cutting themselves off from their rich birthright to accept a miserable mess of pottage.

Then the spinning and the weaving that went on day and night. "Thirty run of hand-spun linen yarn, together with two hams, a bag of potatoes and a barrel of cornmeal,'' was Cicely's contribution to the salary of the minister who preached the gospel at the meeting-house on the hill.

Cicely put into these activities not only the resources, but the wit and even the charm which women of her family in other generations had given to the life of the drawing-room.

Once a committee waited upon her to find fault with her dress. Considering the serious state of public affairs, the necessity for frugality, did she not see that she was setting a bad example by dressing in rich clothes? they asked her.

Cicely listened quietly.

''Since I grew tall enough to wear my mother's gowns I have not had anything new," she said, when they waited for her answer. "It seemed the best economy to use what is in the house."

They said no more, but again, hearing that a dish of tea was always served to the squire in the afternoon, a second deputation came to remonstrate with Cicely upon the use of "the noxious herb," which in these times could only be obtained through unpatriotic sources.

"Let me give you a dish of tea and you shall judge," said Cicely, and before their eyes she brewed a pot and served it to each in a handsome china cup with cream and sugar.

They tasted it grimly, with an air of indulging in forbidden luxuries.

"Is it pleasant and to your taste?" she inquired, archly.

Far too pleasant for honest patriots to indulge in.

Cicely laughed, opened her canister and showed them the leaves.

"These herbs did not grow in China," she said. "You may see me hunting for them like an old witch for her simples. Sage and thyme grow in the garden bed, and I mix with them a bit of catnip, a touch of pennyroyal, and sometimes a little boneset."

Cicely enjoyed her triumphant repartee, but she knew that she had enemies who set these forces working against her, and more than once word came to her that it was Mrs. Marrable and Ruth Gentry who had tried to injure her with the townspeople. But she had her work to do, her duty to her father to fulfill, and if Sidney only kept his faith through this long separation other things might wait.

Morris Marshall, who acted very often as bearer of dispatches between Washington's headquarters and different military posts in New England, always stopped on his way at the Farringtons'. He could talk of the dead boy-soldier. He brought them, besides the news of both armies, the news of the world, and often English newspapers had found their way into his saddle-bags, and gave Mr. Farrington a melancholy satisfaction. Marshall tried as well to make Cicely smile over some of the stories he told her; how when on one occasion his excellency had invited some visiting generals and their aides to a camp-dinner, eighteen in all had sat down to a long table, on one end of which was a dish of salt pork and on the other of boiled beef, between them a dozen potatoes flanked by a few beets; nothing more save a few pies made of green apples. Again Marshall recounted how he happened to be riding with the commander-in-chief when they grew thirsty and stopped at a farm house to ask for a drink from the well. The farmer's wife recognized the general and suggested that she had made some cherry bounce which her husband considered excellent. "By all means, madam," said his Excellency, "Let us drink your good health in the cherry bounce." The good woman ran to bring it, but confusion covered her when she produced the glasses, for they were stamped with the image of George the Third. "I have no others," she faltered.

"Excellent glasses and a very good likeness, I should imagine," said his Excellency, as he drank a bumper of the cordial. "I should like his majesty to know what aid and comfort he has given to General Washington."

It was impossible that Cicely should not feel her burden of loneliness lifted when Marshall came. The state of affairs seemed less wholly grim, desperate and tragic when he gave these humorous touches to his accounts of army life. He never but once spoke of Sidney Marrable; then it was to say that he was the bearer of a letter from the young aide to Ruth Gentry, which he had promised to deliver in person. It sometimes nowadays seemed to Cicely no easy matter to make the idea of Sidney real to herself. Then in such moments, feeling the smart and bruise of such a disappointment as this that Marshall had prepared for her, she would go down the grape-trellis walk, along the garden wall to the shady nook under the willows, and the realization that she loved Sidney and that he loved her would come back with a rush.

Time wore on. A few men who loved ease and a safe hearth better than the turmoil of battle stayed on in Saintford "to protect the women," as they explained. Some of these were a little lukewarm in the cause of independence; others, and Uriel Coxe for one, overflowed with patriotic feeling. If Uriel could have made up his mind just where to concentrate his powers so as to make them most felt he would have enlisted long before.

"There's too many marchings here and too many marchings there," he would say, "to suit me. I'm a goin' to be on one campaign, howsoever, before the final lickin' we give the British comes."

Then again Uriel would exclaim: "Ef I could be commander-in-chief of the Continental army one week," making it clear that the haltings, the manœuverings, the feints, the withdrawings, which had enabled General Washington, even through the direst straits, to keep the field against overwhelming odds, were not to his, Uriel Coxe's, mind. He wanted to hurl one tremendous column on the enemy in New York, he wanted to hurl another tremendous column on the enemy in Philadelphia, and still another tremendous column on the enemy in South Carolina, so that the benighted British should be glad to take to their ships, sail away and never return.

It was supposed that Saintford contained a good many tories. Mr. Farrington and Madam Moulthrop were well known to be over-devoted to the cause of the mother country. There were others who halted, waiting to see which way the tide would turn.

"It reminds me," said Uriel Coxe, "of Uncle Simeon Crane, who, when this colony was just a gittin' settled, was a eating his supper one night when a grizzly b'ar walked in at the open door. Simeon was feared to death o' b'ars, and as his wife, Betsey, was outdoors a-doin' up the chores, Simeon, not havin' nobody to pertect him, jist

clum up the ladder into the loft an,
naterally perferrin' the b'ar shouldn't
foller drawd up the ladder ar'ter him.
Meanwhile Betsey, she cum in, an' a
findin' the b'ar eatin' supper she an'
him had it hot an' merry. Sometimes
the critter was down an' sometimes
Betsey. An' Simeon a-wishin' to be
on the winnin' side ud call out to the
one on top, 'Go it, Betsey,' or, 'Go it,
b'ar,' jest as the case might be.''

Early in July, 1779, Admiral Sir
George Collier and General Tryon, with
two men-of-war, forty-eight tenders
and transports, sailed up Long Island
Sound, made a bid for the allegiance of this waiting tory element,
and Uriel Coxe's long coveted opportunity to hurl ''a tremenjous column on
the enemy'' at last arrived.

On the morning of the sixth of July this proclamation was found nailed up on the church-door:

ADDRESS TO THE INHABIT-ANTS OF CONNECTICUT.

The ungenerous and wanton insurrection against the sovereignty of Great Britain into which this colony has been deluded by the artifices of designing men for private purposes, might well justify in you every fear which conscious guilt could form respecting the intentions of the present armament. Your town, your property, yourselves, lie within the grasp of the power whose forbearance you have ungenerously construed into fear, but whose lenity has persisted in its mild and noble efforts, even though branded with the most unworthy imputations.

The existence of a single habitation on your defenseless coast ought to be a constant reproof to your ingratitude. Can the strength of your whole province cope with the force which might at any time be poured through any district of your country? You are conscious that it cannot. Why then persist in a ruinous and ill-judged resistance? You who lie so much in our power afford that most striking monument of our mercy, and ought therefore to set the first example of returning to allegiance.

Reflect on what gratitude requires of you. If that is insufficient to move you, attend to your own interest; we offer you a refuge against the distress which, you universally acknowledge, broods with increasing and intolerable weight on your country.

We do now declare that whosoever shall be found and remain in peace at his usual place of residence, shall be shielded from any insult either to his person or property, excepting such as bear office, either civil or military, under your present ursurped government, of whom it will be further required that they shall give proofs of their penitence and voluntary submission, and they shall partake of the like immunity.

Those whose folly and obstinacy may slight this favorable warning must take notice that they are not to expect a continuance of that lenity which their insistency would now render blamable.

Given on board his Majesty's ship Camille, on the Sound, July 4, 1779.

George Collier,
Wm. Tryon.

While this proclamation was being discussed by all the townspeople on the village green, Morris Marshall, who had set forth from Saintford at dawn on his way to Hartford, rode back posthaste bringing the news of what had followed the entry of the British fleet into New Haven harbor. The unfortunate inhabitants had been insulted, pillaged, beaten, tortured, slaughtered. Shipping at the wharves, houses and stores, had been burned. The Rev. Dr. Daggett, ex-president of Yale College, had been taken prisoner, wounded, beaten, and in every way outraged.

This was only the beginning of the enemy's depredations, for it was their threat that every village along the Sound which harbored a rebel was to be destroyed.

The news of the indignities offered to Dr. Daggett, who was a kinsman of Cicely's mother, roused Mr. Farrington's indignation. He had not left his house for more than two years, but now, leaning on Morris Marshall's arm, he sallied out and addressed the group gathered before the church-door.

"Men," he said, raising his trembling right arm, "we must protect our homes against—the enemy."

Only Morris Marshall knew by what effort the squire pronounced those bitter words, "the enemy."

"The enemy may arrive off our shore this very day," he went on. "Some of us have wives, some of us have daughters."

"Squire Farrington," said Uriel Coxe, "we will all lay down our lives to save our country."

Mr. Farrington bared his head and looked up.

"We will all lay down our lives to save *our country*," he said.

He had chosen his side at last. He was thrilling with the insult of the proclamation which summoned him back to the allegiance he would have been glad always to hold sacred, which commanded him to reflect upon what gratitude required at the very moment that hired mercenaries were let loose to burn, pillage and torture.

A committee of safety, with Morris Marshall at its head, was organized at once. Every woman in Saintford was advised to pack up her valuables and to be ready, at a moment's warning, to flee toward Danbury. A reconnoissance was made on the Milford shore. No sail was in sight. It was probable that the fleet would move down the Sound toward sunset, and the following plan of operation was decided on: Late in the afternoon Uriel Coxe and his company of Home Guards were to repair to the Point to watch for the enemy, and at the first sign of his approach to light a bonfire which should give the signal. The news would be carried to the village by two men in a row-boat, lying concealed among the sedges of Nicholas Knell's island. Meanwhile Captain Coxe's men were to harass, hinder and delay the landing of the British as long as it was possible.

It was nearing six o'clock that afternoon when the Home Guard set out on their three-mile march, with an ox-cart loaded with provisions. Probably in no campaign of the Revolution was the commissariat so well provided.

"The wimmin-kind, God bless 'em, know that we're a-sacrificing our lives to defend 'em," said Uriel, accepting the substantial tribute.

By seven o'clock the march was ended. The oxen had been turned loose to find pasture. The materials for the bonfire had been gathered. The sixteen men had chosen the place for their bivouac and all was ready. The blue Sound, gently heaving, stretched out on either hand into far-away reaches of pearly haze. Eighteen miles across the watery expanse the shores of Long Island, blue with distance, showed their faint silhouette. Except that every man was armed with sword or musket, some with both weapons, it might have seemed as if everything beneath the over-arching dome of heaven was at peace. The gentle lapping of the waves, the whisper of the breeze through the tall sedges and mulleins, all sang together, making a pleasant lullaby.

The men sat for almost twenty minutes waiting for the enemy, but the enemy did not appear.

"No man can fight on an empty stomick," said Uriel Coxe. "We had better eat a good, substantial meal."

So in default of the enemy, the sixteen men fell upon the ham and tongue and pies. Not that they had left home fasting, far from it, but it seemed a prudent course to fortify themselves.

The sun had set by the time the meal was finished. Lightning began to play on a bank of clouds in the west. The tide was coming in and the waves murmured more and more complainingly. Night advanced apace. Speculation regarding the expected event began to creep into their conversation.

"They can't get into the harbor without a pilot even at high water," said Nathaniel Peabody, in his shrill, piping voice. "It won't be high water till past one o'clock. My idee is they will anchor half a mile out an' send the men ashore in boats not far away from this place where we are now."

The suggestion was unpleasant, still it had to be met. Each man was eager for the important post of bonfire-lighter. The others could draw up into a hollow square, wait for the enemy until they saw the whites of their eyes and then

7

bore it into them; or they could post themselves in the most convenient position and with skilful shots pick off the men one by one as they tried to land. Another suggestion was to scuttle the boats by firing under the water-line. Uriel Coxe thought the best way might be for the whole company to wade out on the shelving sands, meet the boats, upset them and drown the enemy in the surf.

There could be no doubt about this being magnificent, but was it war?

"No shilly-shallying for me," declared Uriel. "I don't want too many tactics. My way is to go straight to the p'int."

The night thickened. The bank of cloud in the west was rising. The lightnings played over it unceasingly.

"I'll warrant," suggested Nathan Brown with a sort of tremor in his voice, "the wimmin-kind at home is a-quakin' an' a-tremblin'."

"Well they may quake," said Nathaniel Peabody, who had barely escaped with his life from New Haven the day before. He went on, his voice growing shriller and more shrill, to describe what he had seen. One tipsy Hessian had eight watches and the sleeve of his coat full of women's trinkets. Then, too, the insults and affronts put upon respectable citizens.

"They called Doctor Daggett a d—d old rebel," he asseverated.

"I'll show 'em if they put in here how a d—d old rebel can beat a d—d old British soldier," observed Uriel.

"S'pose," suggested Nathaniel, "a

company of them men was to start up this minnit out of the tall grass, an' tell us to show 'em the way to Saintford village, a-pokin' their bay'nits into our hind-quarters an' a-telling us to git on?"

"Two can play at that game," said Uriel.

"Ef they wouldn't spare Doctor Daggett o' Yale College what ud they do for plain, 'umble men like us? I tell ye, he begged for his life."

"Not I."

Nathaniel proceeded to describe Doctor Daggett's wounds—four deep bayonet gashes on his skull, three pricks of the bayonets between his ribs; then such a belaboring of his whole body with the barrels of the men's muskets that he fainted dead away.

"Ef I'd 'a' bin Doctor Daggett," said Uriel, "I'd jest 'a' snatched a muskit out'n the nearest man's hands, an' knocked him down, an' while I trampled the life out'n him, I'd jest 'a' struck out an' destroyed every ruffian within reach."

"What was that sound?" somebody whispered.

Distant thunders had begun to mutter. Strange noises came out of the sea, and what was that flash across the face of the waters?

"It wasn't lightning."

"Looked to me like the glim of a lantern. Jest seems to me I seed the hull of a ship. Now, what's that if it ain't the sound o' muffled oars?"

At the same moment, however, their apprehensions were quieted, for an illuminating flash of lightning made everything before them as clear as noonday. There was no man-of-war, no boat, nothing but a black waste of moving waters.

But that sudden clutch of dread had laid hold of every man and was not easily shaken off. They took a snack of bread and cheese and a draught of home-made beer just to pass the time.

Alas, the snack instead of infusing spirit robbed them of it. They grew sleepy. The idea of the British invasion grew far off, misty, improbable.

Even the wicked had sometimes to cease from troubling and be at rest.

Uriel Coxe's patriotism was all that was left. The others' had all oozed out. As he patrolled the beach he felt the natural contempt anyone wide

awake experiences for his fellow-mor-
tals nodding off and snoring. The
storm had gone round to the south.
The late moon would rise toward
dawn; already there was a whitening
of the northeast. The lonely watcher
wished it would grow lighter still;
light enough to clear up huge, shapeless shadows which seemed to be flitting
to and fro over the waters in aimless
circles. Strange, luminous eyes glared
delusively out of these shapes. Uriel
caught himself cowering behind a sand
dune to hide away from these phan-
toms born of fog and mist. Everything seemed to grow uncanny. There
were eerie noises like the rustling of
garments. Not only did the coarse
herbage give out vibrations in the wind,
but something moved—yes, there were

live creatures scuttling through it!
What was it ran across his foot? He
struck at it with his weapon. No matter, the moon would soon be up, and it
would herald the dawn.

Uriel sat down on a sand hummock;
leaning forward with his hands clasping
his musket, he nodded, then dozed.

He woke with a powerful start. Was
that an enemy's bayonet that had
pricked him? He turned shivering.

The moon was up. He could see by
its faint light a row of tall, straight,
pointed weapons—yes, a whole row of
bayonets threatened him.

A blood-curdling yell aroused the
sleepers.

"Scatter, men, scatter!" shouted
Uriel. "We're right amongst the
thickest of 'em."

IV

NOT long after sunrise that day Morris Marshall, after watching all night, brought word to Saintford women that they might light their kitchen fires and prepare breakfast in peace. The enemy's fleet had weighed anchor before dawn, left New Haven behind and, disregarding Saintford, were to strike their next blow farther along the coast. The Home Guard had "scattered" so successfully that some of them, being lost in the woods, did not turn up for a day or two. What had startled the gallant Uriel had been three mullein stalks waving toward him in the rising wind of dawn.

Meanwhile Sidney Marrable had heard of the plundering and burning of New Haven and had asked his chief of staff for a two days' furlough. When he was referred to General Washington, his excellency said he could ill spare anyone just at the time.

"But Saintford, my home, is just in the path of the British," pleaded Sidney.

"Are you married?"

"No, your excellency."

"You have a mother, perhaps?"

"Yes, your excellency."

"A sister?"

"No, your excellency—but—"

"We are hoping to strike a blow presently to our own advantage and the enemy's perplexity," said the general. "The lion going up and down Connecticut seeking whom he may devour is to have a pinch of the tail. But I shall need officers with all their wits about them. I can see that yours are wandering. Accordingly, go find them and bring them back with all possible dispatch."

Sidney had no wish to loiter. He was devoured by anxiety. He set off at once and on his way heard more than once the direful news that the enemy had landed at Saintford Point. Everywhere he came upon men arming, for the militia was rising to go to the defense of the villages along the rivers, inlets and beaches. Sidney finally reached his mother's house just before midnight. Mrs. Marrable and Ruth

were soon roused and could easily reas-
sure him as to their own safety and
the safety of all Saintford. He ate,
drank, went to bed and tossed till dawn,
sleeping only to have a nightmare of
arriving too late to receive his general's
commands. The moment the rose and
gold of the east showed that day was
near he sprang up. He had told his
mother that he would be gone before
she and Ruth were awake. In fact as
far as Ruth was concerned he wished
he had not come. The girl's eyes, her
smiles, her blushes had been so self-
conscious, so triumphant that her very
effort to hide her elation and control it
showed that it had its root in her be-
lief that the young officer had made
this extraordinary journey simply to
assure himself that she was safe and

unharmed. The chief of his concern was for somebody so different even from his mother that Sidney had chafed under the smiles and glances of the two.

It helped him to be out of doors in the fresh, cool wind of dawn. The great thing was to be doing something, putting deed to thought. What he was determined to effect was a sight of and speech with Cicely. He had not seen her all these three years. He stole through the wet grass, crossed the garden and ran down the trellis-walk. The feeling that he was so near her made his blood leap in his veins. He had scarcely spent a thought upon how they were to meet. To stand under her window and look up and let his fancy run riot at the image of the girl lying on the pillow to which he had pressed his lips on that far-away July night, her bright brown hair lying tossed about in sweet disorder, for one long minute, seemed enough. She loved him. The sense of possession passed through him like an electric thrill. Then the call of birds roused him. It was day. Impatience began to stir in him. He flung up a pebble, then another, and called, "Cicely," half under his breath.

There was no answer. It was growing lighter. One moment more of waiting, then he climbed up the trellis and, reaching across the space with his riding whip, tapped softly on the window ledge.

The curtains, which were waving gently to and fro, were pushed aside.

A man's figure appeared. It was Morris Marshall.

"Lieutenant Marrable!" he exclaimed, all the blood rushing to his face. "What are you doing here?"

"Come out, sir," said Sidney, "and I will explain."

Five minutes later the two men were face to face on the grape-walk.

"I wanted a moment's speech with Miss Farrington," Sidney said, with his indomitable, youthful air. "I have ridden more than fifty miles to assure myself that all is well with her."

In spite of his jealousy, in spite of his half hatred of the slim, straight, well-knit young fellow, Marshall's better nature was touched by the signals the handsome face hung out, and the note of feeling in his voice.

"My Cousin Cicely is well," he returned. "She is nursing her father, who has been made ill by the bad news of late, and she is sleeping in the room next his, on the other side of the house."

"She is well, you say?"

"Perfectly well."

Sidney put his hand on Marshall's shoulder. His face worked. His breast heaved.

"Will you tell her," he gasped out, "that the moment I heard there might be danger I could not stay away? I must have news of her. The thought of the enemy in this harbor—"

"Is no relief coming to Connecticut?" demanded Marshall."

"Something is hatching," replied Sidney. "If I guessed what it was, it would be better for me not to say. I am riding back faster than I came. You will tell her I was here?"

Marshall nodded and walked on with Sidney, telling him of Uriel Coxe's gallant campaign. When they came to the place where Sidney's horse was waiting, saddled and bridled, Marshall asked if this worn-out nag could be expected to last through the long ride.

"You are lucky," he observed when Sidney told him his own horse had been resting at Ridgfield since yesterday. "Good animals are getting scarcer and scarcer. Arnold was telling me lately that he had been sending south for horses, but had made out poorly. The British seize and run off

8

every beast they can lay hands upon. 'No horses anywhere,' says Arnold. 'No horses in New York, no horses in Pennsylvania. In Delaware and Maryland they are using mules and oxen altogether, and as for Congress, it is run entirely by donkeys.'"

Sidney, applying spur to horse, laughed as he shouted out, "I will tell his excellency, I will tell his excellency." He rode back with a light heart. Even if he had not seen Cicely he had been near her. Marshall would tell her how he had stood beneath her window and she would guess something of the love and longing which had filled his heart as he looked up. It had given him a quiet, shriven feeling as of having been upon his knees in prayer.

He reached headquarters two hours past noon, and Marshall followed two days later, bringing the news of the destruction that had fallen upon Fairfield and Norwalk. The moment was so serious, so bristling with demands that Sidney found time for but one question, and was contented with Marshall's curt response.

"My Cousin Cicely is well. Mr. Farrington's disorder was mending when I came away."

Sidney had not counted on a message. He was flinging himself heart and soul into the preparations for the attack on Stony Point. This expedition was to be Washington's thundering counterstroke; the pinch of the tail which was to bring the lion back from the Connecticut coast roaring for his more legitimate prey. Anthony Wayne, of whom it was said that where he was there was always fighting, was to conduct the storming-party, and Sidney Marrable was one of his picked men.

"What kind of a post do you like?" inquired the commander.

"Sir," said Sidney, "I like a post of danger."

He was likely to be taken at his word and have his wishes met, so Morris Marshall, who happened to overhear this colloquy, observed to himself shrewdly. The attack bristled with difficulties, some of which were likely enough to be deadly. Sidney had twice made a reconnoissance, and knew every furlong of the way before the detachment of Light Infantry set out from Sandy Beach at noon on July 15th.

The success of the expedition depended on its being a surprise. Not a musket was loaded lest some unwary shot should betray the secret of the march.

"Not a dog must be left to bark—not a cat to mew," said the commander. It was an advance like that of Indian warriors, in single file; what roads existed on that side of the Hudson were incredibly bad, but generally there were none, and the path lay up steep ascents over rough passes, down narrow defiles and through precipitous ravines. Sidney Marrable, who had already tested and prepared for each difficulty of the route, helped to put life and soul into the tedious march; he fell into the step of the surly men and inspired them with hope and good-humor;

he helped one through arduous places, lightened the baggage of another; was ready with canteen and ration.

"The most promising youngster," said Wayne to Morris Marshall, who had come up with General Muhlenberg's column to support the rear of the attacking party if needed, and who crossed the bay in a skiff at sunset to bring a bag of dispatches from headquarters. "He will get promotion."

It seemed to Marshall that every sting, every mortification of his life was called Sidney Marrable. At this moment, besides hearing the young fellow's praises, he was obliged to suffer from the knowledge that his bag of dispatches had contained a letter for Sidney from Cicely Farrington. Marshall stood eying it in the general's hands as a cat a mouse; he would have pounced on it and ground it to atoms had there been a chance. Had he sus-pected it was in his keeping he would have sunk the whole bag of dispatches at the bottom of the river before he delivered it.

"Better not let him waste time and strength reading letters," he said con-temptuously, pointing to the sealed missive.

"I'll wager something it's a love-letter," said the general. "It will put fresh fight into the fellow to have it under his jacket over his heart."

As Marshall saw the light on Sidney's face as he came up to receive his letter, the contraction of his eyes and lips grew dangerous. He stood and waited to see how and when he would read it.

This rendezvous was on the place of a man named Springsteel, a mile and a half below the fort. As the men after their scattered, irregular scramble over the broken way came up, they were given their rations, then formed into columns ready for the attack. Sidney was to lead the van on the right, with twenty picked men; to prepare the way for the advance under Lieutenant-Colonel Fleury.

Sidney looked up at the sky. The dark would come with a stride presently. He must read the letter. He had made an arrangement with a negro in this neighborhood by the name of Pompey, and now, under the pretext of going to meet the man, walked to a little distance, hid himself from view behind a great bowlder, and sitting down used the last precious moments of delay in perusing the epistle which Cicely had written on the very day he had spent in riding toward Saintford to assure himself of her safety. It ran thus:

"Good and true friend:

"Ill news travels so fast you may already have heard of our trouble and perplexity at the British invasion of our peaceful coast. For a whole day we were quaking at the thought that we were ourselves to know all the *horrid chances of war*. By my father's command I packed all our plate, the jewels that belonged to my mother and other valuables. For those few blind, frightened hours of yesterday we ran hither and thither like dumb sheep feeling their danger. To-day we hear from my Cousin Marshall that the enemy has sailed past us, our harbor, perhaps, not being deep enough for their ships. For whatever cause, thank God! My father is ill to-day from the excitement and want of rest. I am writing this within sound of his voice. But, dear friend, I am so light of heart. Although separated from my friend, I feel near my friend. For what separation of distance in miles could be equal to the separation made by my father's hopes being for the cause which is against yours? With his feelings all embittered toward everything American, how could I even let my fancy dwell on any future in which my own happiness had a part? My dearest friend, I have not let myself be daunted. I have gone on as calmly as if I was assured, as cheerfully as if I was brave, as patiently as if I saw before me a bright future instead of one solitary and loveless. But now, dear playmate, I have plucked the very flower of hope out of this time of danger. When my father, instead of saying, 'These rebels,' spoke of 'Our cause against the enemy—' But he calls.

"I hear that dispatches are to be sent at noon. I must close this. I wish for one hour I could be this senseless page —that I could be near you—feel the touch of your hand! Ought I to say this? It is long since we met. Men have been known to change. If you have wavered— But even if you were to forget, it would be sweeter to remember you, unfaithful though you were, than to have the rest of the world true to me.

"From her who has always a prayer in her heart for her true warrior."

For a few minutes in the thrill of it, the joy of it, Sidney forgot where he was. His face was glowing, his heart was beating violently; his hands trembled as he pressed his lips over and over again to the letter, feeling that Cicely had touched it. All at once recollection smote him. He loved his life so well at that instant he was almost a coward. He might be killed to-night. On the edge as he was of the sombre, echoless gulf which had swallowed up many as young and hopeful as himself, Sidney grew thoughtful. He folded the letter carefully in its original folds. Suddenly having a vision of himself lying helpless to be stripped by marauders, he thought with horror that some desecrating hand, some profane eye might alight on this precious page out of the girl's pure heart. He looked about him. With Sidney prompt deed always followed thought.

"If I put the letter under this bowlder," he said to himself, "I can reclaim it—if I survive the battle. If not, in nature's own good time, it will molder into dust."

He kissed the letter once more, then thrust it far under the bowlder into a crevice of the rock beneath. Just then he heard the melancholy note of the whip-poor-will. It was Pompey's signal. Sidney answered.

Pompey had come from the fort,

where he had been selling straw-
berries to the officers. He had promised Sidney to guide the storming-
party across the morass and up the
steep and rocky paths, and he was as
good as his word. The history of that
night attack has been told over and over
again. Sidney Marrable's column was
to move on, remove the abatis and
other obstructions, and surprise the
fort.

"Neither the deep morass," said
General Wayne's report, "the formida-
ble and double rows of abatis, nor the
strong works in front and flank could
damp the ardor of the troops, who, in
the face of a most incessant and tremendous fire of musketry, and from
cannon loaded with grape-shot, forced
their way at the point of the bayonet

through every obstacle, both columns meeting in the centre of the enemy's works at the same instant."

Sidney was shot through the right shoulder just as he entered the fort— one of the first. It was a dangerous but not a mortal wound. Sidney was to live long and prosper—to see his children's children. Nevertheless destiny had stepped in and separated him from Cicely.

Ten minutes after Sidney had hidden the last love-letter Cicely Farrington was ever to write, Morris Marshall, who had watched him, drew it forth from the crevice in the rocks, hesitated whether or not to destroy it, and decided to put it in his pocket.

It does not follow that a man is incapable of remorse because he acts as if he had no scruples of heart or conscience. The spring of Morris Marshall's actions lay not only in his wish to separate Cicely and Sidney, but in his hatred and envy of the young fellow's lithe figure, his every movement swift as an arrow. Marshall waited, hoping to hear that he had fallen. Impetuous to folly, Sidney was always lucky. He was promoted to a captaincy for that night's work, and a little later to a lieutenant-colonelcy.

Morris Marshall contrived that Cicely's letter should fall into Ruth Gentry's hands. He knew that Ruth could fight her own battles.

Cicely never heard of Sidney's ride to Saintford for news of her. What she did hear from gossiping neighbors was that he had come post-haste to assure himself of Ruth Gentry's safety, then had departed within the hour. The cold feeling about Cicely's heart had not loosened its clutch when tidings came of Sidney's gallant doings at Stony Point, and also that he lay dangerously wounded.

Ruth Gentry came to see her one day late in August to bring word that Sidney was better.

"I suppose you will be sending him another letter now," the girl added, with her soft, dimpling smiles.

"I do not understand you," said Cicely.

"Did you write this?" Ruth demanded with a little laugh of derision, holding out the sheet which had already gone through such a singular history. "I couldn't have believed," she went on, "that mistress Cicely Farrington was such a piece of flesh and blood."

Cicely flashed into such a white heat of rage that Ruth shrank, cowered, and when she saw the wronged girl approach her, she flung down the letter and ran out of the house as if she expected to be pursued.

A moment later, when Cicely emerged from her sudden flare of anger, she was alone with the letter; that dumb, accusing witness against Sidney; the sight of which fetched its lash again across her every womanly susceptibility.

Fate was cruel. Letters often miscarried in those times, and the one full of passionate feeling which Sidney wrote while his hurt was mending never reached Cicely. When, after the close of the war, Sidney returned to Saintford Cicely was gone with her father to England to attend James Farrington's nuptials, and there was gossip, perhaps Ruth Gentry knew whence it came, that Cicely was also to make a good marriage there, among their titled relations.

Cicely Farrington never married. But when she came back to Saintford Sidney Marrable was the husband of Ruth Gentry. Morris Marshall could thus be patient, feeling certain that Cicely would ultimately become his wife. Each year brought Marshall fresh wealth and greater honors to offer her, but Cicely said, calmly, she should never marry. She kept her father's house in the old way until, when she was thirty-one years old, he died. Then James brought his wife and child from England. As the new mistress was paramount, Cicely subsided into the place of dependent sister and maiden aunt, and in the stately old colonial house may still be seen the embroidered screens, the tapestries wrought by Cicely's patient hands in the silent years which followed. Modern whist is often played in the drawing-room on a wonderful card-table that she embroidered, with all the fifty-two cards laid out in their bravest semblance.

Sidney Marrable had a place under the government, and rarely came to Saintford, but Cicely used to see Ruth and her and Sidney's children in the pew at church. The summer Cicely was thirty-six she was sitting one day under the trees on the lawn at work, when all at once she perceived Sidney coming across the grass toward her. She rose, a little prim and formal, and looked at him with a white, disturbed face. He was a fine, stately man now. When he held out both his hands, she did not venture to refuse her own to his clasp.

"Cicely," he began without any preamble, "I have just heard from my wife a strange thing."

She only looked her question. He went straight to the point.

"That she once had in her possession a letter of yours addressed to me—that she made you very angry by showing it to you."

"Let it pass—let it pass," said Cicely, faintly. "All that happened years ago."

Still bewildered, he told her how and why he had hidden that letter in a ravine a mile and a half below Stony Point; how even while suffering from the pain and fever of his wound, he had had himself carried to the place afterwards and had found it gone.

"What happened I do not pretend to say," Sidney went on earnestly. "I am the husband of another woman, but if I were not to tell you that I valued that letter, that I value any-thing of yours, Cicely, more than I value my life, I should be helping on the accursed treachery—accursed treachery, I say, that has ruined my life."

"Oh, Sidney, I beseech you—hush—hush!"

"You know it was always so. You know there was never but one woman in the world for me."

"I cannot hear this—"

"They told me you were marrying in England."

"I never had any thought of marrying in England."

"Then I was the more deceived."

For one long moment the two looked at each other. Cicely had grown faded and older, but at that moment all the possible beauty of her youth came back to her face.

He was to remember her thus. He said no more, and presently went away.

Cicely was, perhaps, quieter at heart

after this explanation. However, the passionate pain of those long years had gone deep. She was not well all the winter that followed, but she busied herself embroidering a little robe—like a christening robe. One of the early days of March happened to be singularly warm and spring-like, and Cicely, although frail nowadays, crept forth and with a parcel wrapped in silver tissue took her way over to the Marrables'. Ruth opened the door for her.

"Why, it is Miss Cicely Farrington," she exclaimed. "How white you look! Like one of the snowdrops the children brought in."

"I am not well," said Cicely, "but I felt as if the sun and air might do me good. Ruth, I have brought you a little present for the child you are expecting."

Ruth crimsoned.

"If you could let the dear little creature wear it at the christening," faltered Cicely. "If it should prove to be a girl—if you could let her bear my name!"

Ruth took the little robe and looked at it. It was a marvel of delicate needlework.

It was used six weeks later. By that time Cicely had been in the family vault of the Farringtons about a month. It had needed but a breath to end her life, and she had taken cold that treacherous spring day.

The child that wore the christening robe was a boy. Thus, Cicely's last wish, like many another that had lain

near her heart, never came to pass.
There was no child of Sidney's to bear
her name.

The High Steeple of
St. Chrysostom's

The High Steeple of St. Chrysostom's

I

"YES, an' uncommon pretty young woman she ha' grown too."

"Not old enough for a sweetheart yet?"

"Old eno' an' plenty. Catch sweethearts an' birds a-waitin' for cherries to ripen before they find out they're sweet! Not that Annie cares for sweethearts, though, save as a girl should! I' spite of her dark, wicked

eyes, an' her rare, takin' ways, an' her
smile here an' her word there, no doubt
she is true at heart. Then she's a
proud lass an' comes from a proud
stock; an', till Master Trent came
a-courtin', Mistress Snow had nothing
but frowns for any o' Annie's lovers.
Master Trent's bound to win her, they
say.''

''Master Trent? Joshua Trent, o'
Manor Farm?''

''None else, though he might easy ha'
married squire's daughter an' set up
for a gentleman, but he never had an
eye for any woman alive save Annie.
Mistress Snow ull be main proud to see
her girl at Manor Farm.''

The two men, walking together along
Teddington highway, parted company
here, and Will Ware took the lane which

led past the shadows of the great oaks of the Chase to Farmer Snow's. Will had not been in Teddington parish for three years, but he had forgotten nothing about his early sweetheart. Annie had been but sixteen when he bade her good-by before setting out on his long voyage, yet Will's nimble tongue had already found many a chance to whisper words into her ear which made her eyes droop and her color come, and they had parted with a farewell kiss, long remembered by him with a wild thrill of passionate hope. Now, thank God! that weary interval of waiting was over; he was at home again, and, forty-eight hours after setting his foot in the parish, and greeting his freshly widowed mother, he was on his way to see Annie Snow.

He was still quivering with a curious pain and perplexity over the news he had just heard of a possible rival, when he came in sight of the chimneys of Chase Farm, and the very look of them inspired a sort of comfort which gave him a hopeful view of his own prospects, and showed his and Annie's future in a satisfactory light; and here, just beyond the turning, were Farmer Snow and his wife, driving down the lane in a smart new gig.

"Well, now," said Mistress Snow, whose cold gray eyes saw everything 'twixt sky and earth, "if there isn't Will Ware, as you ha' been frettin' to see! Sit down an' wait, an' what you want'll travel toward you faster'n you can go to it."

"Hilloa, lad!" cried easy, good-natured Farmer Snow, whose stalwart healthiness was a sight to see as he sat in his high wagon, clad in his buff-and-blue Sunday suit, his heavy chin resting on his neck-cloth; "the mistis says, 'There's Will Ware'—an'so it is, an' no mistake!"

"Will Ware, an' no mistake!" cried the young fellow, joyfully, mounting the step of the gig and shaking hands with both husband and wife, and even snatching a kiss from the thin, close lips of Mistress Snow. "You have grown younger and handsomer than ever," he added, looking into her face with his rollicking air and laughing glance. "'Tis the same kiss you gave me at good-by, you know."

"You've lost none o' your boldness goin' up an' down the world," the mistress retorted, her white cheek taking a faint color under the salute. "The master here thinks I'm old enough and plain enough, I'll be bound!"

"I married the handsomest girl in all Teddington, an' I'll not confess as how I've used her so badly that she's grown an old woman at forty," said Farmer Snow, with one of his deep laughs. "So you're back again, Will, an' for good this time, I hear? I was glad when they told me you were goin' to give up sea farin' an' stay home an' take care of your old mother. Teddington parish lost a good man when your father died last winter, but he was failin' fast, an' you can fill his place, since you've come back to take up his trade."

"Yes," returned Will, with a sigh.

"It does not seem the right thing, does it, to leave mother alone, an' she so old, an' I the only child left in her old age? I can't say 'tis my choosin', for I love the sea best, an' I was doin' well. But I believe the Lord's hand is in it all, for parson says so. I had not been at home an hour before Master Brown came in an' told me he had a good openin' for a brisk young fellow who minded no risks, an' would not shrink from danger. 'He needs to be a sort o' sailor,' said he, laughin' as 'twere a joke; then went on to tell that Jem Strong, as he used to depend on for slatin' high roofs and repairin' weathercocks an' water-spouts, was a-gettin' too worthless to be trusted. For a man can't drink his three pints every night, an' double the allowance for Sundays, an' have his eye

sure an' his arm steady in the morning.
So you see, Master Snow, Brown thinks
—as I know a good deal about carpen-
terin' an' the like, that I picked up
along wi' father, as a youngster, an' am
used to sailor's work from bein' a sailor
before the mast for eight years—that
the place might suit me better than any
other. For I'm cool-headed an' steady,
an' no doubt I do understand knottin'
an' splicin' ropes better than landsmen,
an' after my experience in all sorts o'
weather, 'tisn't likely I'm goin' to be
scared by any kind o' climbin', when I
can hold on by my eyelids. Then,
besides, mother feels so thankful an'
happy to think o' my gettin' steady
work in Teddington! There's plenty
o' money to be made by it—not regular
wages, but I shall be paid by the job,

an' liberally too, as a man ought to be
who risks his life."

"Lucky now that you was such a
handy boy, an' larned the trade,"
observed Farmer Snow. "An', I dare
say, you had a chance to keep your
hand in at sea?"

"Indeed I did. 'Twas always said on
board the Helena that I had a better
eye an' a quicker hand than the ship-
carpenter; an' the captain, he told me
once I could make my fortune as a
rigger."

"You'll never lose a chance o'
makin' your fortune by any extra
modesty, Will Ware," said Mistress
Snow, tartly.

The young man's face fell.

"What have I bragged on?" he asked,
looking from one to the other with a

troubled glance. "Next to my poor old mother, I seem to have a right to expect interest an' kindness from my old friends."

"Oh, lad, the mistis will have her joke," said the kind farmer, laughing, but with an uncomfortable air, while his wife's grim face did not alter. "Were you bound to the farm? We can't turn back to-day, even for an old friend like you, Will."

"Is Annie home?" inquired the young fellow, sheepishly, the blood rushing to his face.

"Annie is busy," said Mistress Snow, curtly. "Come again, Will, an' we'll all be home an' welcome you gladly."

Will stepped to the ground and watched the pair drive off. For a few moments his heart was heavy as lead.

Were they changed, or had his own
over-eager, over-hungry heart demanded too much? Must he consider his
journey at an end, his visit postponed
until another day, with the house in
sight, and Annie almost within sound of
his voice? Even if she were busy, it
was not likely her occupations could be
arduous on this Saturday afternoon;
and, if she were finishing a new bonnet
or gown for the Sunday, might he not
sit by her side and tell her what would
be most becoming? He regained his
audacity, and instead of turning back
strode jauntily on. The great farm-
yard gate was wide open, and he entered
and stood looking about him, renewing
with delight each old homely impres-
sion, and feeling as if he recognized
even the tiny ducks and chicks, like

balls of fluffy down, obediently following their mother's sharp cluck. A
monster turkey-cock, alone in his glory,
strutted and gobbled; a long line of
ducks solemnly followed their leader
from the pond; half a dozen calves in
the paddock approached the bars and
sniffed toward him hungrily; while the
great mastiff chained to his kennel
watched the intruder with a cautious
eye.

"Giant, is that you?" said Will; and,
with a joyful bark, the dog threw himself on the young man, licking his face
and whining. It seemed to Will a good
sign to have such a welcome from Annie's own dog, and he went forward and
knocked at the open door of the great
kitchen of Chase Farm.

Mistress Snow was well known to be

the best housekeeper in both Great and Little Teddington, and the perfection of polished brightness, and the repose of a full week's accomplished work, reigned in her kitchen this Saturday afternoon. The rows of pewter dishes and pans shone like silver; the brasses were brightened into mirrors, which reflected every ray of color and light; while tables and chairs showed that a stout hand had rubbed them to their cleanest that morning. A young maid-servant sat at the open window, sur-reptitiously putting a fresh ribbon in her Sunday bonnet in the absence of her sharp-eyed and sharper-tongued mis-tress, and at the sound of the knock came running to the door.

"Is Miss Annie Snow at home?" Will inquired, with some trepidation.

"She's in the laundry-yard, a-gath-
erin' the damask-roses, sir," answered
the little maid, looking with admiration
at the sailor's tall, well-knit figure,
bronzed face, blue eyes, and clustering
brown curls.

Will had regathered boldness from the
unchanged aspect of the farmhouse,
and, telling the little maid that he would
go out to her young mistress, strode
across the black-oaken floor of the
kitchen, and went through the scullery-
door to the garden; for well enough he
remembered where the damask-roses
grew. It was a pretty spot; the grass
was close-cut, and grew soft as velvet;
on one side a hedge of privet separated
it from the kitchen-garden, where all
sorts of summer vegetables were ripen-
ing in the June sunshine; and on the

other hand the long dairy-house in-closed it from the farm-yard. Then, in front, were the great rose-trees, which were Mistress Snow's boast and pride, and to-day they were in full blow, and made a superb bank of color with their multitudinous crimson, pink and white petals massed against the vivid green-ery; and there—

"Gathering flowers, herself the fairest"— stood Annie Snow, with her apron full of damask-roses.

Even had there been no other reason, Will must have checked himself for a moment's gaze at this pretty sight. A sheet of snowy linen lay spread over the grass, upon which was piled a pyra-mid of the roses, while Annie was still occupied in pulling more from the half-stripped bushes. Will had remembered

155

the young girl's beauty with a weight upon his heart and tongue for many a year; but she had grown a woman since he saw her last. Her hair no longer clustered in the curly crop he remembered, but was neatly braided; yet nothing could alter the delicate little curls and rings which shaded her forehead and temples. Her eyes were as dark as her hair, or seemed so from the shade of the thick, black lashes; but one could hardly tell what was their color, for when Annie looked she held the man she looked at under the spell of her gaze, and he was helpless, and not until she smiled with tender curves of the beautiful lips, and droll little dimples, did her victim gather heart. Just at this moment Will could not tell whether she were more absorbed in gathering roses or listening to a dark, stern-faced man who stood close beside her, whispering occasionally some trifling word, while his eyes fastened, as if insatiable, upon the young girl's rounded, babyish curves of cheek and throat. Her apron was full of the fragrant petals, and, as she turned to empty them, she caught a glimpse of Will on the porch, and uttered a cry. He strode forward, and, between her surprise and his seizing her hands, the apron dropped and the roses fell to the ground.

Annie bent her head with a devouring blush, and said, faintly, "I dropped the roses!" and they both went down upon their knees, and began picking them up. Will had found one chance to gaze into the depths of Annie's eyes, and dis-

covered there a fire which leaped to
meet the blaze in his own. But nothing
could be said before Joshua Trent, who
stood regarding them both sullenly;
and, accordingly, the sailor, scrambling
to his feet, turned and greeted his
rival.

Master Trent wasted no graciousness
upon the intruder, but Will gave small
heed to his lowering glance and forbid-
ding air, and, giving him not another
look or thought, turned back to Annie,
whose cheeks had gained a color more
delicious than the hue of her own
roses.

"You were gathering these for the
linen-closet just before I went away,
Annie," he said, softly. She looked up
at him without a word, but he knew
that she remembered the day he had

kissed her for the first and only time. "Did you know that I had come home, Annie?" he said again.

"Yes," she answered, under her breath. "Father told me how you had come home."

"I should ha' come to see you yesterday," Will pursued. "But there's many a thing to be settled at home—father being gone, you know."

"I was sorry—I thought of you—I went to see your mother," faltered Annie, with a timid glance of love and pity.

"Bless you for your kindness!" cried Will, rapturously. "Mother never told me."

"I hear," broke in Master Trent's rasping voice—"I hear that you have been discharged from your ship, an'

will have to earn your bread in Teddington henceforth?''

Will stared at him.

"What d'ye mean, man?'' he asked,
shortly.

"I mean what I say,'' retorted Trent,
with a grin. "You be discharged, ben't
you?''

"Oh, have it your own way. I certainly
have my discharge in my pocket, an' I
hope to earn my bread and more too in
Teddington,'' said Will, too happy to
feel exasperation at such an innuendo.

"I didn't hear what they brought
against you,'' pursued Trent, "but I
knew you was discharged.''

Will glared at him a moment; then,
finding resentment out of place, turned
back to Annie, and, leaning over her
shoulder, helped her to pick the roses,

throwing them into her lifted apron, while he whispered over and over his raptures at meeting her. Once his cheek touched the little pink ear, and they started apart guiltily.

"I'm afraid you're not entertained, Master Trent," said Annie, returning to a consciousness of her double duties, and remembering the claims of her rebuffed suitor, who stood glooming in the background. "But then you know Will Ware is an old friend, an' I've not seen him since I was grown up."

"Oh," rejoined Trent, with an effort at a smile, which was rendered hideous by his rage coming in collision with this sudden necessity for politeness, "I can wait until Will Ware goes. Your mother asked me to stay to tea and supper, Annie."

11

"You'll stay too, Will?" she cried, looking up at him.

. "No," said, he gravely, remembering his repulse from Mistress Snow. "I came only to have one look at you, Annie, an' to bring you a few poor keepsakes I picked up in foreign parts. I'd like to stay if your mother had asked me, Annie," he added, looking into her face and sighing. Her loveliness stirred so maddening a thrill that he experienced a powerful, almost painful emotion, when her full glance answered his. He thrust his hand into his pocket and brought out his little presents, just to hide the rush of feeling which came over him.

"I've brought you a queer fan, Annie," said he. "It smells o' sandalwood, an' you may like it. An' here's some shells from Ceylon, and some ivory carvings from China and Bombay, which may make you laugh, they are so queer. An' here's a sort o' pocket, such as the Indian women make in America."

He tossed them one after another into her lap as she sat on the bench.

"I've another present for you, Annie," he whispered in her ear, "but that shall wait."

Here he half drew a little ring with sapphires from his waistcoat pocket, then slid it back.

"Since 'tis the fashion to give presents in public," observed Master Trent, advancing with a sour, disagreeable laugh, "I'll take this opportunity to give you a little box wi' something in it for you, Annie, which may have cost as much as Will Ware's trumpery, although I didn't go so far for it."

"I make no gifts to a girl who counts their cost in counting their worth," cried Will, hotly. "But let's see Master Trent's present, Annie, an' we'll guess how many golden guineas he paid for it."

Annie was used to being *casus belli* between her lovers, hence cared little about these defiant sarcasms, and sat meanwhile holding a brilliant conch-shell to her ear with the naive wonder of a child at the roar. But, as Trent handed her his offering, she dropped the shell and took the little box, smiling and blushing as she looked up into the grim, yellow face. Then she threw Will a glance which convinced him that in spite of all these coquetries she cared nothing for Trent; and at last, after toying daintily with the little casket of purple morocco, opened it with a kittenis hair, and then shrieked with rapture.

"Oh Master Trent, I never did see anything so beautiful."

For on the satin lining lay a chain and locket of gold. The mind of a pretty girl is thoroughly subjective. For Annie to see beauty in any shape was to long to appropriate it to her own adornment. A flower was not half a flower until it nestled in her throat or hair. Hence now, after one glance at her costly present, she drew it out, and with a swift movement and arch smile clasped the necklace about her throat, and the locket, bright with blue enamel and set with pearls, hung down the snowy neck half exposed by the square cut of her bodice.

Each man gave a start. Will blushed jealously, while Trent's face lighted as he remembered that it was his locket which rose and fell with every breath of that tender breast. But neither spoke, and Annie's vain little heart sank, for she had expected flattery from both.

"You might just say if I look nice in it!" she exclaimed with a pout, as little understanding the gush of feeling which exalted both her lovers as a new-born babe understands the rapture of its mother's kiss. "Do I look so ugly, then?" she asked Will, with a little grimace, and, springing up, his presents slipped from her lap, and were scattered on the grass. "Don't mind, Will," she said, coaxingly. "I'll pick 'em up presently, but now I want to run to mother's room an' see how I look."

"I'll tell you how you look, Annie," cried Will, snatching her hand—"you look as if all the beautiful things in the world were made for you; not that they make you prettier, but that they show a man how beautiful they are when you wear them. Still, all the same, Annie—"

"But what, Will?" she asked, as he broke off. "What were you going to say?"

"I like you best i' your plain gown with a rose in your hair. Nothing can make a rose more beautiful—no, not if it stands in a gold vase."

"For my part," said Master Trent,

with elation, "I like to see a woman bravely rigged out. My wife shall wear the handsomest silk gowns in Tedding-ton—the ladies at the Chase shall not be finer. I'll put money in her purse, to let her buy what she will."

But Annie was not listening. She was standing beside Will; his hand still clasped hers, and his look and touch moved something in her heart stronger than either vanity or coquetry. Presently her little fingers went up to the necklace, unfastened it, drew it off, and laid it back in the box.

"Thank you for giving me a chance to try on a real gold necklace, Master Trent," she said, offering it to him with a little courtesy.

"No, no, Miss Annie," he answered, with a gruff laugh. "You'll keep it, if you please, with many happy returns, for your birthday, which I know comes to-morrow. Mistress Snow herself gave me leave to present it to you."

Annie stood looking down. She could bear without a sign of emotion the news that a strong man loved her, but she was frightened at the thought that her mother might scold her. She was recognizing too late the annoyance entailed by her general habit of coquetry. She wished that she had never allowed Trent to believe for a moment that his visits to the house were welcome to anyone except her mother; she wished, indeed, that no man in the world had ever thought of her except Will, so that there need be no clashing of old duty with her new inclinations.

"Good-by, Annie," spoke Will, breaking the silence which only the bird's twitter and the farmyard noises interrupted. "I'll see you after church to-morrow if the weather is fine."

Annie smiled faintly, and at his motion her little hand flew toward his, and nestled in it. He drew her with him across the grass-plot, all the time whispering in her ear until he gained the shadowed porch. He was no laggard in love, and found time all in this moment to tell his story of passionate longing, to gain her answer in return, to steal a kiss from her lips, and to put his ring of sapphires on her finger.

He left her with such a tumult at her heart, and such blushes on her cheek, that Annie dared not go back to Trent at once, so called to him that she must get out the blue china, and lay the cloth for tea against the return of Mistress Snow.

II.

WILL WARE belonged essentially to the class of lucky Lochinvars, and could woo and win a wife and carry her off, if need be, under the very eyes of his rival. Joshua Trent, on the other hand, had none of those parts about him which carry captive a girl's fancy. He was dark and stern in face, shackeled in movement, with a voice which could not attune itself to gentle meanings, and, above all, a mind which, however quick in defining its own needs, never expanded into real sympathy with another's. A long line of cold, narrow-

natured progenitors had made him what
he was, and thirty years of exacting
selfishness had rendered him powerless
to conquer the despotism of his sullen,
gloomy disposition. No thrill of awe
before God, no pity for his kind, had
ever linked him in bonds of hope and
sympathy with other men; he experienced no sense of dearness or nearness
when observing the exquisite pageant
of Nature, and cared nothing for the
crystal dome of sky, the lake, now blue
as hyacinth-bells, again glassing a chaos
of storm-driven clouds, nor the oaken
glades where lights and shadows played
endlessly. Yet dull and blank although
his mind was to what we term in general its finer uses, he was endowed
beyond other men with a powerful
capacity of feeling for his own wants,

and all his ardor of imagination, otherwise suppressed, had spent itself in his love for Annie Snow. He had loved her since she was a child, and this experience had undoubtedly been a check upon other ambitions and interests. She was but fourteen when his eyes first kindled into admiration at sight of her; for the first four years he never once spoke to her, yet watched for hours to see her pass along the lane, and knew by heart the ribbons that she wore—the very buckles on her shoes. He was no coward, but a schemer, and could hold grip over his heart and tongue while he bided his time, and thus continued to work himself into Mistress Snow's good graces long before he asked her consent to his paying his court to Annie.

Mistress Snow had been a coquette in her youth, and, as a woman of middle age, her self-love had taken the shape of ambition and avarice. Now, the Trents had held Manor Farm by honest title for upwards of three hundred years; and the old house, half farm-house, half gentleman's manor, had many a fine tradition of the thrift and wealth of by-gone Trents. Many a proud marriage had these vanished generations of Trents made, and many a boast might Joshua vaunt of his high relations in the next county. Hence, when Mistress Snow learned that the young man wanted Annie, she felt that such a marriage would suit her aspirations for her only child. She had given a ready consent to Joshua's suit, and had not been slow in influencing her daughter toward him. Yet, with all the prestige thus gained, the lover made haste slowly.

Many a present of fruit and vegetables, and game, came to Mistress Snow from Manor Farm, and once all the Snows spent a day at Trent's house, and viewed with admiration, tinged with awe, the wide hall, rich wainscots and carvings, black with age. Then Mistress Snow and Annie had enjoyed glimpses of old presses filled with treasures of linen they well knew how to value, and they had looked into the great kitchen, with its fireplace large enough to roast an ox whole; while Farmer Snow could not half express his admiration of the farm outside, with its well tilled fields and woods, the full garners, and the horses, cattle, and poultry.

Annie knew very well that she might be mistress of all this wealth if she but gave her hand to Joshua Trent. But in her heart she thought the house gloomy, and her spirits shrank at the picture her imagination was swift to present—of herself chained there in her bright youth; sitting in those quaintly-carved, high-backed chairs; sleeping in the vast, melancholy bed, where grim Trents had died generation after generation; presiding at that long, funereal table, with Joshua opposite, only less yellow and hideous than his father's picture above him on the wall. For girls have swift divinations when they do not love a man, and, though keeping their minds in the bounds of maidenly thought, may yet foresee with exactness all the aspects of married life. Before

Will Ware's return there had been moments when, wholly under her mother's influence, she believed a life with a rich husband like Trent not wholly unendurable. But Will's glances, and Will's clasp of her hand, had been a magical test; all that was false and artificial in her nature vanished under the power of this new feeling, and she instantly ceased to think of Trent save as a disagreeable shadow in the brightness of her world.

What she did think of was Will—his looks, tones, and words, at their last meeting; his returning on the morrow; and, now that he had come, a quality softer, gentler, lovelier, had developed in her face and manners; a sort of dependence and clinging to something stronger and better than herself, which

179

was met and fully answered by his manly tenderness.

Joshua Trent was not slow to discover this change in Annie, and he watched her altered manner to himself, as she shyly withdrew from his proffered attentions, with a steadily increasing jealousy and wrath. He observed, too, that he had lost the ear of Mistress Snow; true, when he did insist upon addressing her privately upon the subject of Will Ware's attentions to Annie, she had said that she knew nothing; that the master would let his only child choose the man of her heart; that things must bide their time; that nobody could tell what romantic folly lay at the root of a girl's mind, let her training have been what it might. All of which Trent listened to with a look on his

sombre face, and a contraction of the
muscles about his mouth, and a motion
of his hands, that led Mistress Snow
much into Annie's way of thinking that
he would never make a kind husband.
In fact, pondering the matter, she told
herself with relief that, although Will
Ware came of humble stock, everybody
knew him to have the sweetest temper
of any man in Teddington.

One afternoon, late in August, Annie
Snow was returning from a tea-drinking
with friends in the next parish. Some
of them had walked with her half-way,
but at the stile, just before crossing the
great meadows beyond the Chase,
Annie bade them good-by, and, skirting
the fields of rye, now ready for harvest,
she turned into the quiet lane which
led toward home. She had picked a

handful of poppies as she came through
the rye, and had put a knot of them in
her dark, shining braids, and another
on her breast. She was walking slowly;
and, as she advanced, swinging her
bonnet in her hand, made a picture fair
enough to fire any lover. She was loit-
ering a little, because it was not yet
seven o'clock, and Will could not meet
her at the great oak until it had passed
the half-hour. Thinking of the coming
interview, she was in a mood of happy
reverie, and to Trent, who had been
watching for her since six o'clock, and
now beheld her approach, she seemed a
maddening vision of beauty. Although
for an hour he had been hiding in the
coppice, straining his eyes in every
direction in the hope of seeing her, now
that she did appear in full view, the

sight filled him with a burning, shuddering pain akin to dread. His glance
fastened upon her as if he were under a
spell while she unconsciously advanced.
She seemed to have gained height and
breadth of late; her form was magnificent, and the elastic pride of her step
seemed cruelly beautiful to the man
who felt his hopes trampled beneath
her feet.

She drew nearer; there was the pure
white forehead, with the delicate rings
of curls about it. Trent saw the poppies in her hair, and the flame they
made upon her breast. With a beating
heart he emerged from his covert and
drew near her.

"Good-evening," said she, opening
her dark eyes with a look of surprise,
yet speaking as if she were too deeply

engrossed in thought to be aroused from her reverie.

"Good-evening, Miss Annie," he answered, coolly, walking beside her. "Perhaps you'll be glad of my company along this lonely lane?"

"No, thank you!" she returned with spirit. "I am well used to going alone, an' can take care of myself. You are far away from your own home, Master Trent, so I'll bid you good-night."

"Maybe you're expecting some other sweetheart," said Trent, his face growing black. "But stop one moment, Annie Snow. To my mind, a man like Joshua Trent, of Manor Farm, has some rights over the woman he has been courtin' for more'n a year! Perhaps I'm not so patient as you think! I want a wife, an' I want her now, an' if it so pleases you, we'll have the banns called next Sunday."

Annie regarded him scornfully.

"You must be dreaming, Master Trent; or, if you're joking, no man should dare to joke o' having his name called wi' mine."

He looked at her silently raging; she could hear him grind his teeth.

"By —!" said he, under his breath, "you shall marry me, Annie Snow! I'm not the man for a girl to fool with— accepting his presents, going to look at his house, an' all. You shall marry me, I say!"

She laughed insolently.

"Did I want your presents?" she cried. "Go gather fruit from our trees, and make up your poultry from our farm- yard. As for your chain an' locket, you

know very well I never took it—
mother'll be glad to give it back to you,
You know I told you that over an' over.
so 'twas your own fault for leaving it
behind you."

She was so fair in her scorn, while
her cheeks flamed high as the poppies
in color, that his love smote him to sup-
plication.

"O Annie," said he, going up to her
and speaking under the influence of
strong emotion, "I did think you were
beginning to like me! What else have
I thought of these five years that's
gone? I ha' not set out a tree, nor
marked one to be cut down, nor
counted my lambs, nor weighed my
wool, nor called home my cattle, but
what I ha' thought, 'All this is for
Annie Snow to take.' I ha' thought of

you every spring at planting-time, I ha' thought o' you in the heats o' summer, an' more than ever in the fall as I sat over the fire, until in winter-time there was naught else to do save to think, 'Some day she may be here.' . . . I tell you, girl, you can't get over facts like these. I am thirty years old, an' ever since I was five-and-twenty I ha' made up my mind to ha' you for my wife. Before mother died she called me to her an' said, 'Joshua, thee must take a wife now.' An' I told her, 'I'm a-waitin', mother, for the time when Annie Snow grows to be a woman.' An' she died believing you were to be mistress o' Manor Farm. . . . An' it must be so, Annie. You can't begin to guess what it is for a man to put his hope in a girl for five whole years! All

187

his thoughts learn to tread one path, and
that toward her; an' that path burns
deeper into his soul every day, an'
month, an' year—for to go on seeing
her, thinking o'the time she is to be his
wife, makes him half mad in his joy at
her beauty. . . . An'—an'—an'—you've
been good to me, Annie, most times;
an', till Will Ware came home, I never
doubted for a moment that you were
sure to marry me when the time came!"

Annie had gazed at him awed, almost
stupefied, by this sudden show of vehe-
mence, and she was terrified, besides,
at the working of his sombre face,
which in its grief and passion grew
unfamiliar and grotesque. But, when
he came nearer with his arms out-
stretched, she withdrew, with her air of
girlish caprice.

"I never heard," she said, haughtily, "as how a girl is to blame if a man makes up his mind against her wishes that he wants to marry her! Five years ago I was fourteen, an' I never thought then o' marrying you, nor did I think of it last year, nor do I think of it to-day—thanking you all the same for believing me to be a fit mistress for Manor Farm—which is a house for a girl to be proud of, if she wants to marry a house, an' farrows o' pigs, an' droves o' cattle, an' cribs o' corn!"

"'Twas but to show I was backed by something fit for you to take that I talked o' Manor Farm," interposed Trent, humbly. "An' if you marry me, Annie, you shall live like a lady, you shall, indeed! an' shall have a carriage with two gray ponies like the young ladies at the Chase."

Annie gave a light laugh.

"I'll not say, Master Trent," she returned, easily, "that I should not like to live like a lady, an' be idle all day, an' drive about after a pair o' long-tailed gray ponies; but"—here she sent him a swift glance which thrilled him from head to foot—"but," she went on, with a sudden intensity of look and manner, "though I may like to have all things easy and pleasant, I would rather work my fingers to the bone for the man I love, than to sit on a gold throne with a crown on my head, an' have a man I didna care for as my husband!"

Trent was trembling under the fervor of her words and the passion of her face. He caught her in his arms.

"You shall be my wife!" he muttered, with a terrible oath; "you shall be my wife, let it cost me what it may! I'll risk anything before I let you go away free to marry another man!"

He tried to kiss her, but she was little less powerful than he, and with a convulsive wrench she escaped him, darted to a safe distance, then flung back a few rankling words:

"I marry you, Master Trent! I'd marry the ploughboy sooner—sooner yet, I'd die before I'd be your wife!"

She flew down the lane with a spring like a startled doe, and Trent was left fixed and motionless as if turned to stone. In his heart and mind he felt the inner tempest of strong feeling, and knew what it was to be alive, to suffer, to long, to despair. He was unused to

emotion, and this impotent desire
goaded him like a bull. He felt the
girl's beauty with a thirst, a fury of
admiration; all his long, patient waiting, all his repressed but ardent hopes,
glared in upon him, mocking him with
the misery of his humiliation and his
loss.

For twenty minutes after she left him
he stood just where she had torn herself
from his arms, fixed, every muscle rigid
with the frightful pain he was experi-
encing. All at once he started. He
heard a whistle, and divined instinct-
ively what was to happen. He stooped
and picked up a scarlet-beaded pocket
which he had torn from Annie's belt in
the struggle, and turning a little from
the path leaned against a tree. In
another moment Will Ware appeared

around the turning of the lane, walking rapidly, with his hands in his pockets, and whistling "When the Bloom is on the Rye." He stopped short as he saw Trent, and gazed at him with astonishment and curiosity. Trent, as if unconscious of anyone's vicinity, was pressing his lips with frenzy to the scarlet pocket he held in his hand.

"How are you, Mr. Joshua Trent?" said Will, dryly. "Pretty well wrapped up in what you're doin', eh? I happen to know the owner of that trifle you hold in your hand. I expect you picked it up here in the lane."

Trent had turned with an affectation of sullen surprise. "Good-evening to you," said he, curtly, and stuffed the pocket inside his waistcoat.

"I'll trouble you for that pocket,

Joshua Trent," cried Will, with plenty of determination in his voice. "I know very well the person it belongs to, an' 'tis but fair for you to give it up at once. I bought it myself from an Indian woman in Canada, an' you, certainly, ha' no right to it."

"The best right of any man alive," responded Trent, with a hideous leer.

"The right of a thief!" said Will, hotly. "Give it me this minute, or it shall be the worse for you."

Trent laughed insolently, and sat down on the rock with his legs astride. "Here's a pretty mess," he ejaculated, with a chuckle. "P'r'aps you'd like me to render up everything my little black-eyed Annie ever gave to me."

His face and mien added fuel to Will's anger.

194

"She has given ye nothing but bare civility," said he. "I know your purpose, Master Trent, an' 'tis unworthy an honest man. Gi' me her property, I say. I ha' the best, the only right to whatever is hers."

"What right?" demanded Trent, coolly.

"The right o' her promised husband."

"Her husband!" shrieked Trent, with a grin. "You can't be such a fool, Will Ware, as to go to her for a wife. Buy her more cheap, an' seek an honest girl if you want a wife. Annie Snow's beauty might redeem a trifle o' lightness, but such lightness as hers ought to damn even her beauty."

Will stood a moment motionless, staring at Trent with eyes in which amazement turned slowly to fierceness as the meaning of the words smote him like red-hot missiles. Trent continued to look at him with his fiendish grin, and, taking out poor Annie's pocket, gave it a caress.

At this sight, possessed by a frantic rage, Will tore it from him, and, brandishing his fist in his face, bade him take back his words.

"You lie, you false, cowardly scoundrel!" he muttered, in a stifled voice. "Take back your words, or I'll crush your head against the very stone you're sitting on!"

"If you want to fight," returned Trent, rising with the bound of a tiger, "I'll fight you willingly. But for a light o' love like Annie Snow—"

Trent had no chance to add another word; all his strength was needed to parry Will's blows. For a few seconds neither yielded; then Trent, tired of acting on the defensive, and watching for an opportunity, flung himself on Will, and the two men, closing on each other, wrestled with the fierceness of panthers. The struggle was short. It was not long before they fell to the ground, and Will was uppermost, with his hand on the other's throat.

"Don't kill me!" gurgled Trent. "I take it back. 'Twas but to fool you. I picked up the pocket."

Will withdrew his clutch reluctantly; his wrath was fully aroused, and he felt his vengeance still unwreaked.

"Lie there, you cowardly scoundrel!" said he, rising and looking down at his opponent, and kicking him contemptuously—"lie there until I am out of sight,

and don't come within a mile of Chase
Farm again, or I'll finish what I have
only begun to-night—I swear, by heaven, I will!''

III.

TRENT'S insane outburst of jealousy had the effect of such unguarded outbursts, and defeated his own schemes of separating the lovers.

Annie never heard of the fracas among the tall ferns in the summer twilight, but Will told her parents, and in consequence they withdrew every semblance of opposition to his suit, and allowed him to press for an early wedding-day, which was fixed for the third week in October. Mistress Snow had looked forward to her child's wedding-day ever since her birth, and no German Fräulein was ever better provided with hoarded stores for her outfit than was Annie. Then, besides the counting out of linen, and flannel, and damask, at the farm, there was the new home to be provided with everything befitting, and many an afternoon in September did the farmer's wife spend with gentle, helpless, deaf Mistress Ware, who was but too glad to yield to every suggestion of the thrifty dame's.

"For, after all," remarked Mistress Snow, on her return, "the house is not so bad, though Will's mother is too easy an' comfortable a creature to make the best of what she has. You'll soon get things to your liking, Annie, even if there be but five rooms, an', if you haven't a great waste o' spare-rooms, an' store-rooms, an' dairies, an' the like, the less the care of 'em will make an old woman of you by the time you are thirty. Then to see the clever little contrivances Will sits up half the night to work out makes me half ready to fall in love with him myself. I doubt not but what you'll be a happy wife, Annie. There ha' been times when I was ambitious for my only child, but now I like to think you're sure to marry a good an' just man, besides being the handsomest young fellow in all Teddington," the mother added, smiling and stroking the soft hair of the happy girl whose head lay across her breast.

Many a rough joke had Will to parry or endure in these days, but he was both too happy and too busy to care what was going on in the world outside his own hopes and efforts. He proved a swift and careful workman, and had found plenty of occupation in Teddington, and now was busy repairing the high steeple of St. Chrysostom's. It was a job which had been waiting three years for a good workman. Many a man had come from other towns, looked at the high tower, shaken his head and gone away. There was plenty of risk; life or death must depend upon a single rope, upon the steadiness of head, eye, and hand; and the man who undertook it must peril his life as does the soldier his in battle. So the timid had said, but not Will Ware, who had not a drop of coward's blood in his veins. Yet he was never reckless; he was careful about every inch of scaffolding, and allowed no man to touch his ropes but himself.

"Don't fret, Annie," he said to her

once as she told him her fears; "I'm as safe in the spire as you are here, my pet. Let them tell you, if they like, that, when they look up from the market-place, I seem like a fly crawling about the steeple. That's very likely. But don't think I love my life so little as to take no precautions. Indeed, 'tis a joke at the shop about the time I spend over my ropes. Be sure I keep my senses hard at work lookin' out for danger."

Thus secure, it was not a hard fate to Will to spend his working-hours far above the sweltering heats of summer and early autumn—above the coarse jokes of the shop, and the poor hilarity, the hard thoughts, and the rivalry. So, one September day, a little door far up in the tower of great St. Chrysostom's

—looking to the gazers down in the market-place hardly bigger than a man's hand—opened. Bats and owls flew out into the sunshine; then a human head appeared, and a pair of stout arms, which soon made a flying scaffolding—tier after tier, ladder after ladder—until the top of the spire was reached.

It was there that Will Ware had worked for many a long day alone, bound by a cord to the pinnacle, descending lower and lower as his hammer fastened on the slates with swift, heavy strokes. It seemed to him, these fleeting, early autumn days, that he was very near to heaven; the sky was to him softer and bluer than when seen from the lower earth; wavering, gleaming apparitions of clouds floated by like angels flying on their lovely missions; street-sounds came to his ears made musical by distance, and the swallows twittered about him all day long. When the summer waned, and the swallows flew toward the eternal suns, darting forth an arrowy swarm darkening the air, Will shouted glad adieux to them. Well he remembered that their flight was no date for him by which to mark coming darkness and winter, but rather the joyful premonition of his glowing season of delight. Let them fly toward the summer lands; let the leaves blaze into gold and scarlet, then fade, and fall, and mould! Will had no dread of the shortening days and chilling nights. No wonder if he felt near to heaven in these times; no wonder if his glad heart made glad and easy work as he thought of his approaching wedding-day!

The tall steeple of St. Chrysostom's rises from the tower in a single unbroken line into the sky; but at the base, where it joins the buttresses, is a double row of pinnacles and turrets, which change the sober majesty of the great church, relieving it with an aspect of lightness and beauty. These pinnacles had first been made of stone, and beautifully enriched at the angles and parapets with crockets and gargoyles, in those old days when pious hearts rejoiced in quaint and careful work as their dedication to the Lord; but the light and friable stone had not well stood the battle against wind and weather these three centuries and more, and had crumbled dangerously, until the partial restoration of the church, when turrets and piers were replaced by plain designs in wood and slate. This work had been so badly executed that every storm ripped off the slates, and sent them clattering down among the gravestones below; and replacing these, and repairing the leaden spouts, was now, of all Will's undertaking, the part which presented most difficulties.

As we have seen, his ready contrivance had robbed the extreme height of the spire of danger, and the gradual swell had afforded him constant aid. But now, below the turrets, he might fairly be said to be suspended 'twixt heaven and earth. To have built scaffolding would have taken away half the profits of his enterprise; hence he had for weeks studied the situation from every point, until he made certain that he could accomplish his work without support from below. No one understood knotting and splicing better than Will. His inch and a quarter ropes were first made fast to the staircase inside the spire-light, next "reeved" by blocks and pulleys to the window casement. Then, with a stout "cable" about his waist, and twice slung over his shoulder, he could, by the aid of another rope, swing himself up and down between the window of the steeple and the pinnacles of the tower with the ease and lightness of a bird on the wing. It was a triumph for him thus to accomplish his work alone and unassisted. Never had he felt more proud over a day's achievement. Afterward, when he went home through the dusk, he found Annie wait-

ing for him in the thicket of rose-bushes
by his own gate.

He saw her spring out, then retreat,
as if frightened at her own boldness; so
what could he do but gather her into
his arms?

"What are you doin', Annie?" he
whispered.

"Mother's in the house," she answered. "I waited for you, Will. I
durst not go in alone. Your mother'll
talk of you, an' I blush; then I feel
ashamed to be so foolish."

But Will found such folly adorable,
and told her so. They walked around
the little garden hand-in-hand and arm-
in-arm.

Then Will took her into the street
and along the town to the market-place,
to show her how nearly finished was

the high steeple of St. Chrysostom's.
Annie shuddered as she thought of
Will swinging there all day. She hated
the sheaves of slender spires which had
hitherto been something to look at with
delight. So she told him as they gazed
up at the turrets of the tower, so delicately, almost transparently, limned
against the pale evening sky. Then,
as they went back together, they encountered Joshua Trent, who passed
them scowling, seeming to see them
not.

"Ugh! it makes my flesh creep to
meet him," whispered Annie. But
Will laughed.

"He can't hurt thee, my darling."

It had long been settled that Annie
was to have one look at her new home
before coming to it as a bride, and Mis-

tress Snow had brought her over on this Wednesday after dark, that the gossips of Teddington might not discover her visit. The two mothers watched the young people walk over the house after supper. Annie was very shy, and Will very proud as he showed what he had done for her comfort and convenience; still, the thought of their swiftly-approaching future pressed upon him as it did upon Annie.

"Do you love me, Annie, half as much as I love you?" he asked her.

"I love you next to God, Will!" she said, throwing her arms about his neck.

He held her close, his face working, his heart overwrought with strong emotion.

"Tell me, Annie, what you love me for," said he again.

"For shame, Will!"

"But tell me, Annie. I love you because you have a trick o' looking at me, an' pullin' heart, an' strength, an' sense right out o' me; because if you speak I can do naught save to follow you, an' if I even but touch your little hand I am undone unless I can kiss these sweet lips, an' be a man again."

"You must not love me for such things, Will," expostulated Annie, blushing deeper and deeper. "Love me because I am going to make you a good an' pious wife."

"I love you in all sorts o' ways," said Will, soberly. "But why do you love me?"

Annie laughed.

"I dunno. I ha'n't a good reason, Will," she said, roguishly. "P'r'aps

I've a foolish reason or two like your-
self. You're none so ugly, an' you are
straight as an arrow, an' strong as an
ox, an' have a way wi' you as if nothing could conquer you."

"Oh, what a foolish girl!" cried
Will, triumphing over her to his
heart's content. "I doubt if there's
much wisdom between us both."

    *   *   *   *   *

Words are no symbols for the fury
which the sight of Will and his bride-
elect, and the sound of their careless
laughter, roused in Joshua Trent as he
passed them in the gloaming. Many a
time in the few past weeks since he
knew that Annie was irremediably
lost to him, his passion of imperious,
impotent longing seemed at last to be
dulled, deadened almost, by the in-

tensity of his accumulating hatred
against the girl who had repulsed his
suit, and the man who had taken her
from him. To live on, bearing this
crush of insults without opportunity for
revenge, seemed impossible; he suffered, for a few moments after passing
Will and Annie, all the tortures of the
damned. His face was convulsed, his
deep-drawn breath came from a breast
heaving with agony. He felt that he
must hide himself from the eyes of men,
for he could not stand upright; his knees
almost failed under him—cold drops of
anguish stood on his brow. He was
passing the church, and staggered into
the shadow of the tower and sat down
on the steps. Above him was the
luminous sky, just touched with color
from the after-glow in the west. The

stars came out and hung golden over the market-place, and a tender little new moon shone down into the purple shadows of the church-yard. It was an evening full of the peace of God, but Joshua Trent felt neither rest, repose, nor hope—nothing save the wretchedness of insane jealousy and thwarted passion . . . . He was almost bereft of reason. . . .

He was recalled to realities by the touch of a man's hand upon his shoulder, and, looking up, saw old Bede, the sexton, with a lantern in his hand, grinning in his face, and ready to shake him roughly for a vagrant.

"Ef I didna think it wur some drunken fellow from the ' Three Crows!' " ejaculated Bede, in his shrill, wheezy voice. "An' 'tis Master Trent!

Anything wrong, belike, that you're sittin' here wi' your head on your hands?''

"No, no!" returned Trent, sullenly. "I'm waiting for nine o'clock to strike to keep an appointment. Go on; never mind me, if you are going inside, Bede.''

"I can't get into the belfry till Johnny comes wi' the key," returned Bede, testily. "Parson he forgets hissen keys, then comes to me ef he wants to show a gentleman over the church. Parson he'll laugh an' say: 'Bede, I've forgot my keys. Just gi' me yourn, an' I'll be sure to hang 'em on the nail in their place as I come back.' An' then parson he's so absentminded he forgets, an' I has to send Johnny trotting up to the parsonage after 'em."

Accordingly, Bede sank down heavily upon the steps beside Trent, who felt powerless to rise and move away.

"Ain't there but two sets o' keys?" he inquired, indifferently.

"Three. Will Ware has the others now that he's workin' on the steeple. Keerful ever is Will Ware. ' Bede,' he says to me every day, ' doan't you let a soul up the belfry-stairs, or I'll carry you up an' throw you out the bell-tower!' He must ha' his joke, you know, Will Ware—he's allus so good-natured. But he says, an' says true, that ef he once knew there was man, woman, or child in the belfry, he wouldn't feel safe a minute."

"What a fool!" ejaculated Trent.

"Not so much a fool. 'Twas none so bad high up on the steeple, for he'd slung a rope round the very pinnacle, an' had a scaffolding besides. But ha' you seen him to-day on the turrets? He's made hisself a little car of ropes that he pulls round—but there's no footing. Domned ef I'd do what he does for a thousand pounds, an' marry Farmer Snow's daughter into the bargain! You'd think it a ticklish job, Master Trent, ef you ever see how he managed! He has to fasten his ropes to the steeple-stairs, an' he must not leave an inch o' cord to meet a sharp edge, for ef a single twist was to cut, and the rope wear loose and slack, down he'd fall a hundred feet and break his neck on these very stones here! He takes his hammer an' twenty slate or so, an' lets hisself down, an' there he is helpless. Let me leave the door

unlocked, so that some domned mis-
chievous boy could go up and touch
them ropes—who knows but what in
five minutes handsome Will Ware 'ud
be lyin' here all a shapeless, horrid
mass, as Annie Snow 'ud die rather'n
look at!''

"Any rope is liable to break," said
Trent.

"Not when Will Ware has tried it,"
returned Bede, rising. "Thank ye
kindly, Johnny. What did parson tell
ye?"

"Parson said he forgot," said Johnny.

"Jes' so. Now, Johnny, run home.
—It's hard on nine o'clock, Master
Trent. Good-night to ye. I'm goin'
up to toll the bell for the dean. My
lady will have it tolled all noon-spell;
as if 'twasn't enough to have all Ted-

dington ha' lost their relish for their dinners, she must ha' their dreams spoiled by tolling it at curfew too. Good-night, master."

"Good-night, Bede."

The key grated in the lock of the stout mediæval portal, which swung wide, then shut with a clang, driven to by the draught down from the belfry-tower, as the sexton opened the inner door.

Any one who saw Master Trent's face in the dusk would have believed he had listened to some joyful news. Ever since he had fought with Will Ware in the lane, he had gone about begirt with terrible, nameless thoughts. If he passed the black tarn in the hollow of his three hills at Manor Farm, he had a vision of a dead man lying there,

the pallid face glaring up with eyes
vacant to all the show of earth and sky.
Wherever he went the thought of vengeance haunted and waylaid him,
pointing to coverts where he might
wrestle once more with his mortal
enemy unseen—devised every mode
and fashion of horrid death. But
these had been vague and formless
fancies. It needed a darker climax of
misery like this to-night to precipitate
these aimless dreams, and give him
suddenly this clearer vision. No
sooner had Bede left him than his
mind, as if lighted by a thousand minute
tapers, illuminated the course before
him, stretching out to a cruel certainty.

He started to his feet with a stealthy
spring, and something in the glitter of
his eyes sharpened his likeness to a

beast of prey. Above from the belfry sounded the wild, sweet note of the death-bell tolling, tolling, tolling the tale of earthly sorrow to the calm evening skies. Each stroke of the bell smote Trent like a blow as he stole along. He experienced an unconquerable dread, as if, in place of working out his own doom, he were caught instead in a silent whirlpool from which he was powerless to escape. He felt cut off from living, breathing humanity, which hoped and prayed with ardent heart-throbs; he was encompassed by his cold, sullen fury. Still, he wished the bell would cease. The sound must make angels look out from heaven, and demons gaze up from hell, who would see him as he crept into the vestibule, entered the belfry-tower—

which Bede had left unlocked — and crouched shuddering under the stair-way.

IV

ANNIE SNOW could not sleep that
night, but lay smiling and glowing the while, hearing in thought and
dream alike all that Will had said to
her that evening. When dawn looked
rosily in through the white curtains of
her bed, she roused herself, and turned
to see the October hazes hanging heavy
over the great woods of the Chase,
and watched the gladsome light of day
flinging itself down with a joyful leap
from cloud to hill-top, and from hill-top
to valley, which it lit with strange
gleams of color as the night-fogs rose
with the curls of smoke from the cot-

tage-chimneys, and vanished into the
blue. It was pleasant to Annie to see
the day appear, to behold the lines of
the forest unfold higher and higher
from their curtains of mist, and show
their mellow tints of gold, and crimson,
and olive, and russet to the first sun-
beams which made them unfurl before
the awakening breeze like a gorgeous
banner.

Annie was of no use to her mother
that day; she was preoccupied with her
great joy, and saw her familiar sur-
roundings as in a dream.

"Since you have no brains to-day,
my girl," Mistress Snow said, at last,
half impatient of her abstraction, "and
since the morning is wasted for you
anyhow, go to the buttery an' choose a
pair o' chickens, an' put 'em in a

basket, and take 'em to Nancy Jones,
an' tell her I wish her joy o' her son's
return, an' send her something for
his supper. Poor, shiftless body, she
ne'er had a thing on hand for a man to
stop his hunger with. Go now, Annie,
an' when you come back, we'll take a
bit o' dinner an' start off early to your
aunt's. 'Tis fitting that you should
see all your relations before Sunday.''

Annie obeyed her mother, and set
out on her walk at once. The mastiff
whined as she crossed the farm-yard,
and, unloosing his chain, she answered
his caresses until he was ready to follow her soberly down the lane. She
walked slowly; she was to-day in such
an enchanted world of dreams that the
voices she heard were faint, the sights
shadowy. She was thinking endlessly

of Will's words — she was looking in imagination at his face.

At the turning of the lane she was arrested by a voice, and, stopping, saw a man rising out of the tall brakes and advancing toward her. Although he did not speak, his face startled her.

"What is it, Master Trent?" she faltered.

"What time o' day may it be, Annie Snow?" he asked, with a smile — the smile of a foeman who takes sure aim and sees his prey fall.

"It is almost eleven o'clock," she answered, with a sort of reserve, yet continuing to stare at him as if fascinated.

"Then you've got no lover but me," cried Trent, with hideous elation. "I told you I'd have you, let it cost what

it might, an' now you can take me.
You needn't stare at me so. I never
did it. It all happened by chance. I
did nothing—nothing—nothing! But
for all his knotting, and twisting, and
pulling the great ropes, they were sure
to cut on the sharp ridge of the window!"

As the man spoke his breast heaved
and labored; sweat stood on his brow
in great beads; he seemed to be gazing
at some horrid sight.

Annie's heart almost died within
her.

"What has happened?" she shrieked,
convulsively. "What have you done
to Will Ware, Master Trent?"

"Done? I've done nothing," he returned, and burst into frightful laughter; then, as if his mind were in a

chaos, he began to rave about a man on the dome of St. Chrysostom's steeple looking no bigger than a fly from the market-place — of displaced pulleys, of cut ropes and dangling cords, and a shapeless, horrible mass, which she would die rather than look at, on the stones below.

Annie had flung down her basket with a scream of agony, and set off with the mastiff by her side.

"It's too late!" Trent cried out. "It's an hour too late. It was sure to happen an hour ago."

She heard him not. She was already out of the lane, and had reached Teddington highway. The safety of what she loved best hung on the swiftness of her flight; yet, though she sped like a deer, it seemed to her that her feet were clogged. She could not think, even if she had dared to think, for her heart hammered so wildly in her ears. One landmark was gained and passed. The Chase woods stopped at the lodge-gate. The road grew alive with riders and equipages. She turned aside for nothing. Everything drew back for her as she was seen rushing on like one distraught. Men and women, turning pale as they recognized her in her frantic flight, stared in amazement, and followed her with a thrill of curiosity and terror. She was in sight of St. Chrysostom's. She gave a great shriek of joy. Could she trust her eyes? For surely a something hung from the steeple. She could see a net of ropes dangling there, and that black object below was surely a man. Her feet gained wings; she sped still faster.

The great market-place in front of St. Chrysostom's was full of people. Fifteen minutes before some lounger there had said to a passer-by that he could not understand what ailed Will Ware. He had dropped his hammer and a dozen slates on the pavement, and they had made clatter enough to wake the dead. Something was wrong, perhaps—but what? Will Ware was no fool to risk his life by a false step or a loose rope. Yet something seemed to have slipped. So another man stopped to gaze curiously up, then two, then twenty; and by that time, with a feeling that something was wrong, help was sent to the belfry-tower, and the lock of the door was discovered to have been tampered with so that the key would not turn. The door had to be broken in.

Outside the crowd gathered and gazed — the parson out of his study, the shopkeepers, the street-loiterers, the women and children. A man with a field-glass had raised the thrill of curiosity into a deeper one of horror by observing that Will had lost all support from the ropes about his shoulders and waist; that he was hanging without a chance of footing, his left hand only clinging to some flying cord which either slackened or gave way from its support, and stretched lower and lower every moment. What he was doing now was swinging himself cautiously toward one of the buttresses beneath, that he might jump as the rope gave way.

By this time three hundred different faces, all pale as if frozen by one Medusa touch, were upturned in this general paralysis of stony horror. Now and then a murmur or a groan was heard, otherwise there was not a sound. They almost feared to breathe, as each man trembled and quivered with terror where he stood. The fifteen minutes seemed a lifetime; they held a suspense which made it an eternity.

Then suddenly arose a hoarse murmur.

"They're there at last!" shouted fifty voices, in a simultaneous, frantic yell, and the terrible calm of dread broke into storm. Two faces had appeared at the narrow door far up the steeple, and every one knew that the men carried lengths of heavy rope. It

had been an interval of such helpless-
ness that at this chance of rescue the
gazers gave out a voice of thankfulness
which rose in a jubilant roar.

Before the tumults had swelled to
their loudest, they were silenced by a
woman's shrill shriek. The rope by
which Will held had slackened, as the
last strand cut through, and, to save
himself, with one strenuous exertion of
strength he swung down toward the
buttress, held a moment, then fell full
forty feet, but fastened by an almost
superhuman effort to the pediment
above the high façade. Here he strove
to keep his balance, clinging with feet
and hands to the carved *basso-rilievo*.
It was of no use. Before one dared
draw breath, he had fallen fifty-six
feet, and lay on the church-steps below,

and a girl was kneeling by the shapeless mass.

*   *   *   *   *

"You had better take her away,"
said the doctors. "He is not dead, but
will never revive. The moment we
move him it will disclose some horrible mangling."

"She has fainted," observed the parson. "Bear her to my house, my men,
then let us attend to this poor, murdered fellow."

"Ay, murdered! I heerd her say, as
she flew 'cross the market-place,
' 'Twas Joshua Trent cut the ropes!'"

"Joshua Trent has killed the best
man in Teddington, be the other who
he may," howled forth one of Will's
fellow-workmen, in clamorous grief.

They raised the crushed, helpless body, put it on a shutter, and bore it down the street, inside the gate, across the threshold into Mrs. Ware's cottage, and laid it on the bed, freshly decked that morning for the wedding-couch. Then every one went out on tiptoe save the parson and the surgeons. Outside all Teddington gathered, breathless, voiceless, waiting to hear the fiat which would shortly come forth that Will was dying.

"He will never be conscious again," was the first whisper which ran around, and men unused to tears burst into wild weeping. The church-clock on St. Chrysostom's tower struck twelve—struck one—two—three—and the crowd outside the little house still stood watching, waiting, and fearing. Will was still alive, his heart beat faintly, but his brain was crushed in; he might live for days yet, it began to be murmured from one to the other.

Four o'clock. The great London doctor who had come down at noon to see Sir John, at the Chase, descended from Sir John's carriage, threaded the crowd, and joined the council of doctors by the bedside. Five o'clock from St. Chrysostom's. The great London doctor emerged, talking to the parson. The parson said, at the carriage-window:

"You will send him down at once, Sir Peregrine?"

"The operation shall be performed at nine o'clock to-morrow morning."

The parson, flushed and excited, and quivering with hope and relief, tells

his chief parishioners among the crowd
that it is thought "trepanning" may
save Will's life.   One of the local surgeons comes out in such good spirits
that he can make a joke about the case.

"Enough fractures to need a whole
college of surgeons.   A student would
have a chance to master everything at
once."

*   *   *   *   *

A week went past in Teddington.
No hammer rang on the church-tower,
and people had not yet gotten over a
trick of looking up and shuddering as
they passed St. Chrysostom's; but the
first excitement had lost its hold upon
the town.   Will Ware's fellow-workmen, as they went day after day to
their places, where furnaces roared,

engines boomed, or skilled hands wrought out their labor, had but time to stop and ask Mrs. Ware:

"How's Will this morning?"

"He lies an' moans, poor lad; but we think he begins to take notice."

"Annie Snow's wi' him?"

"Always. I can do naught for my boy; her eyes are so keen, her ears so swift, an' her hands so willin', she does everything for him. An' to remember their weddin'-day's past in this way!"

"He'll never get up," the men would say to each other, with a shrug. "Better for him to ha' been killed outright. He's but twenty-four, an' to go to the workus—"

"Teddington people'll never let Will Ware go to the workus."

"But as a man has a long life to live —people forgets. They'll raise him a hundred pounds, maybe; then something else'll turn up. He'll lie an' suffer, an' long to die, an' pretty Annie Snow'll take another sweetheart."

V.

IT was Christmas-eve in Teddington. Brief daylight had they had that day, for "the silent snow possessed the earth," and night had closed in early.

"The yule-log sparkled keen with frost,
No wing of wind the region swept,
But over all things brooding slept
The quiet sense of something lost."

Will sat bolstered up in bed. A log blazed on the hearth, but there was no light in the room save the wavering, vermilion gleams of fire-flush on the low walls. Mistress Ware slept, softly breathing, in her easy-chair. Annie Snow knelt on the hearth-rug playing with the kitten, yet feeling her heart

243

heavy with perplexed sadness. Once she lifted the closed curtain and looked out; snow was still falling. It was to be a white Christmas, and people had said all day that if the storm did not abate by nightfall there could be few carols sung this year.

"Annie," spoke Will, scarcely above his breath.

The girl sprang joyfully to obey his call. Not once had he spoken her name like this during all his long illness. He had never asked a service save of his mother, although poor, deaf, placid Mistress Ware could do nothing for him. Annie knelt beside the bed and looked up with the attitude of a willing slave, who says, "Lord, I am here."

Will's own face was in shadow · but

he could plainly see her glowing cheeks and shining eyes—almost too plainly for his self-control, for, although she was worn and wasted, never had she seemed so beautiful to him.

"What is it, Will?" she asked, oppressed by the silence which made her tremble and burn with some nameless dread.

"Annie," he answered, in a broken voice, "I heard your mother telling you to go home with her to-day. What ailed you, not to go?"

"Do you want me away, Will?"

"But I need your watchin' an' waitin' no longer, Annie."

"An' who is to take care o' you, I should like to know?" Annie burst out, passionately. "Who would sit by you at night as I do, never sleeping so sound but what I can hear you move, and so moisten your lips wi' the drink, an' give you the powders? Who would keep the fire bright, an' bring your hot broth every hour? An' who would look after your bandages, an' loose 'em when they hurt you, not waitin' for 'em to grow so tight as to give you pain? Your mother would do it all if she could; but she is old, an' her ears heavy, an' her sleep so sound—it takes a stout shake to wake her."

"Granny Thorpe would come, Annie."

Annie gave some exclamation; and, starting up with some of her old impetuosity, went back to the fire.

"Come to me, Annie," whispered Will.

She yielded to his entreaty, and returned to the bedside, but stood apart from him.

"I'll stay the night, Will," said she, with a tremor in her voice. "I canna get away in such a storm. Father'll take me home after church to-morrow."

He knew by the sound of her voice that she was crying. He stretched out his right arm, and drew her toward him.

"Annie," said he, looking into her face, "ye know what the doctor says."

"Yes," she returned, shy at the touch, and trembling at the look upon his face.

"I shall be a cripple always," said Will, without any weakness in his voice. "P'r'aps more—p'r'aps less— but always a cripple. My chest may get over its weakness when I grow well and hearty—my left arm'll never be no good any more—an' there'll be many an ache in my head. What a poor fellow I shall be, Annie!''

She could not speak, but her shyness and pride were all absorbed in womanly pity. She laid her cheek on his.

"He did it for me that day," pursued Will, with a sigh. "If Joshua Trent—"

"Don't speak his name!" cried Annie feverishly. "I can bear it as coming from God, but not as coming from that man. When I think o' him —it all breaks on me with a rush; I can't bear it. Then to have him get away so quiet that nobody could find him an' punish him!"

"I'm glad they never caught him,"

said Will, quietly. "I've suffered enough — God knows I've suffered enough—I want no other man to suffer —not one—not even Joshua Trent! An', besides, 'twas all because he loved you, Annie; an' I know—I know that for a man to give up the woman he loves dear, is hard—harder than suffering or death."

He clasped her close with his good right arm, and bowed his head upon hers; then said, after a long pause:

"But we was happy, Annie. We should ha' been most happy if it could ha' been. But 'twas not to be."

She gave a cry, and nestled closer to him.

"You don't love me any more, Will," she said, with a burst of tears. "Your sickness has changed you. I've heard it happens so sometimes. You don't love me any more! I've seen it all along ever since you first began to take notice, but I would not let myself believe it! I thought you must have a little feeling for me that 'ud come back when you got better!"

He pushed her away from him.

"O God, help me!" he muttered. "Annie, you don't know what you are sayin'! I mustn't tell you the truth! I must not. Not love you any more? If you only knew, Annie! But I must not tell you!"

"An' why not, Will? What is it that has come between us?"

"Am I the man you promised to marry, Annie Snow?" he burst out, vehemently. "Am I the same man who courted you last summer — who

kissed you—met you in the lane—
walked home from church wi' you?
Could I look your father i' the face, an
ask him to gi' *me* a wife? *Me*, a miserable cripple, weak, useless, wi' but
one arm, no power in head or body to
earn a livin' for my wife—to say
naught o' makin' a livin' for the
children who would come! . . . Annie,
I durst not make so bold—I durst not,
I say! You must go home — the
sooner the better— I'm not worth the
touch o' these little hands! Somebody'll take care o' me—but better that
nobody should help me to live—better
if I'd die—if I'd died the day I fell!
I've knowed it all the time! I had no
right ever to open my eyes again!''

Annie was terrified lest he should
do himself a mischief in his passion.

She passed her little hand across his face.

"S'pose, Will," she murmured — "s'pose it had been a month later when it happened, an' I was your lawful, wedded wife? What then? Would you ha' sent me away?"

He drew her down upon his breast. In spite of his despairing renunciation, a thrill of joy had run through him.

"You couldn't ha' gone then," said he. "I do believe, Annie, you want to marry me just as I am!"

"I would not think," retorted Annie, laughing and blushing as their full glances met—"I would not think o' marryin' a man dead set against having a wife."

* * * * *

All Teddington went to St. Chrysos-

tom's Easter-Monday to see Will Ware
hobble down the aisle with his bride
upon his arm, and such kissing and
handshaking had never gone on in the
vestry-room as now ensued after the
pretty, blushing bride had written her
name in the great book. Farmer
Snow was there with smiles and
laughter, and his wife with a tear in
her eye; and all Teddington knew that
Annie and her husband were to live
with the old people at the farm, and
that Will was to succeed to all the
duties of the place. For Will was no
wreck of a man—there is no irreme-
diable wreck and ruin save in the heart
and mind; and since he had kissed
Annie that Christmas-eve, with the
wild, sweet kiss of their second be-
trothal, he had felt in heart and mind

the strength and aspiration of a dozen men.

    *   *   *   *   *

When the bride and bridegroom had driven away with Farmer Snow, the crowd did not disperse its various ways, but still lingered about the church-yard. Knots of men and women clustered in every corner, discussing a strange piece of news. All these months it had been believed that, since Joshua Trent had stolen up the stone steps of the belfry-tower to do his cruel work, the vengeance of God and man alike had slumbered, and the criminal had gone free. But now all Tedding-ton was to hear that this very morning —away over in the hollow between the three hills behind Manor Farm—there had floated to the surface of the black tarn a terrible thing; and thus it was revealed that the would-be murderer had felt the horror of his accursed deed so strongly that he had ended his life there.

THE END